ORDINARY WORLD

Also by Mike Attebery

The Grimwood Trilogy:
Flares
Ordinary World
The Midnight Visitors

Four Corners Thrillers:
Chokecherry Canyon
Firepower

Brick Ransom Thrillers:
Seattle On Ice
Bloody Pulp
Billionaires, Bullets, Exploding Monkeys

Standalone Novels:
On/Off
Rosé in Saint Tropez

Ordinary World

Mike Attebery

Cryptic Bindings
Seattle

For Ashton G. Eldredge
and Leo Mandrakos

"Love is for the living."

Year Two

Timeline

1855 – Town of Grimwood is settled.

1869 – Ashton Grimwood founds Grimwood University.

1921 – Alan Grimwood is born.

1945 – Grimwood graduates and begins teaching at the University.

1955 – *Revenant* is published.

1969 – Founding of The Grimwood Writing Center.

1972 – Shooting on Grimwood campus.

1974 – *Black Robes* is published.

1978 – Alan Grimwood dies.

1981 – Grimwood's books go back into print.

1983 – Excerpts of *Doppelganger* are published.

1984 – *The Collected Stories of Alan Grimwood (1950-1978)* published.

...Present Day

1.

HEAT WAVES RIPPLED OVER the sidewalk as Brooke ran down the street. Her breath was hot and dry, the taste of rust scorching the back of her throat as she rounded the corner of 76th and started for Greenwood Avenue. She always turned before she passed those stairs. If she had her way, she'd never lay eyes on them again.

She took a left at the next corner and picked up the pace. The heat of the pavement burning through the soles of her sneakers as she passed The Dean Apartments, dodged a lady walking her poodle in front of Perkins Green, and jogged to a stop in front of Racquet Club Apartments – the ramshackle complex she'd called home since she returned to Grimwood in July.

Brooke hadn't felt right in the city. Her parents were there. The people she'd once considered her friends were there. But she no longer fit in that world. Her first week at home, she would lay awake in the dark, feeling the air pressing down on her.

She wasn't the same person. Life had worn her sharp edges smooth. The casual barbs of the city now cut her in ways they never had before. And her mind was somewhere else… Returning to Grimwood was risky, but the path out of her grief seemed to run through the place where everything had changed. So she'd come back to town in the heat of the summer, to experience Grimwood the way Jason might have, and to figure out where and *how* she went on from there.

Brooke rested her hands on her waist as she strolled along the fence-line, feeling the edges of her hip bones beneath the sinewy layers of muscle. Running was new for her. It wasn't even something she'd *decided* to take up. The second week back, she went out for a midday walk, and found herself moving faster and faster as the images came flooding in, until she was flat out running, fighting like hell to get ahead of the memories that washed over her at every corner. Afterwards, she realized the sweat and the pain were therapeutic. Now she ran every day – always when the sun was at its peak – pushing herself to her physical and emotional limits. All these weeks later, she wasn't sure if her mind was at peace, but physically, she'd never been in better shape.

As far as student apartment complexes went, Racquet Club was a notorious shithole, with dilapidated buildings, leaky roofs, plywood stairs that crunched beneath matted olive carpet, and the lingering sense that The Rats of Nimh were living in the basement. It was also the only place she could find a furnished apartment on short notice.

Cathie Pepper had invited her to stay at the house, but Brooke wasn't up to it. She did however find it surprisingly comforting to visit her late boyfriend's mother from time to time. They seldom mentioned Jason by name, but he was always present in the pauses in their conversation. Cathie Pepper was beginning to fill two voids in Brooke's life, straddling the line between a mother figure and a friend.

Brooke wiped the sweat from her brow as she cut across the patchy crabgrass in front of her unit. She pulled the screen door open with a creak, and was surprised to see the front door sitting open.

"Good morning," Loren said, as she stood over the kitchen sink, slurping milk from her cereal bowl.

"You're up early."

"I couldn't sleep," Loren said.

Not long after she'd found the place and signed a short term lease, Brooke was surprised to find her roommate was still in town for the summer and working at the bookstore. The moment she'd mentioned the spare bedroom in her rundown apartment, Loren had asked if she could split the rent with her.

"What time did you get in?" Brooke asked as she sat on the floor to stretch.

"I think I left Cole's place around eleven."

Loren was still dating Cole Phillips, and spent several nights a week at his apartment, but Brooke sensed her roommate needed some space lately. That was fine with her, as it provided some welcome distraction from her own thoughts.

"Something on your mind?"

"I don't know…" Loren said it in a way that suggested both an answer and a question. Then added, "You're looking *strong*."

Brooke arched an eyebrow. "Is that a good thing?"

"Absolutely."

"Then I'll take it. I sure as hell needed *some* kind of change. I suppose compulsive running is as good an option as anything else. I couldn't keep hanging around this place all day watching *Judge Judy*."

"Speaking of change, any idea when we can move back to campus?"

"Are you as sick of this place as I am?"

Loren nodded. "I never thought I'd be so anxious to get back to the dorms."

"Classes start in two weeks, so it's getting closer. When does everyone else get here? Have you heard from Hannah?"

"Not yet, but you know how she is."

"What about Braden?" Brooke asked carefully.

Loren rinsed her bowl and set it in the dish rack. "No word from him either."

"Does he know you're here?"

"Not that I'm aware of," she replied before quickly changing the subject. "I might walk up to Student Housing later and see what I can find out."

"See how many times you can mention the name *Racquet Club*. Maybe they'll take pity on us and push up our move-in day."

* * *

Student Housing showed them no pity, but they *did* give Loren a definitive date, one which she circled on their calendar in purple marker so she and Brooke could count down the days.

Hank and Hannah arrived the day before move-in, planning to stay the night in Brooke and Loren's living room before they all moved back to campus the next morning. They arrived at the apartment in the afternoon, shortly after Brooke's run. She could hear them dragging their bags in the front door as she was getting out of the shower.

"You made it," Brooke said as she stepped out of the bathroom in sweats and Jason's old TOOL shirt.

Hannah gave her a hug. "Damn, Brooke, you've gotten buff!"

"That's what Loren keeps saying too. Was I like a pillow person before?"

"Of course not, but you've brought it up to a whole new level. And you let your hair grow out!"

Brooke ran her fingers through her damp hair, "I guess I did. How are you guys doing?"

"Pretty good," Hank said as he cast a wary glance around the living room. "This place is… interesting. How long have you guys been here again?"

"Fifty-seven and a half days. Not that I'm counting or anything. But don't worry, you only have to make it through one night."

"What is this, like a zombie movie?"

"I wouldn't say zombies are a problem so much as cockroaches."

A look of horror flashed across Hannah's face. *"Shut up."*

"I wish I could. Loren will tell you."

"And what room are we sleeping in?"

Brooke nodded toward the floor. "Unless Loren stays at Cole's tonight, I'm afraid you're looking at it."

"This could be a long night, Hank," Hannah murmured.

"Then we should spend as much time as possible *someplace else.*"

"Like… at a hotel?" Brooke asked

"No, I mean like bowling or The Shack. *Anyplace* but here. No offense, Brooke."

"Believe me, none taken. That sounds like a plan to me. I'll call Loren and see if she can join us. Any idea when Braden gets in?"

Hank shook his head. "You know Brady. He just shows up."

~

No one was surprised when Loren arrived at The White Russian alone. She didn't even feel the need to explain Cole's absence, she just went around the room welcoming everyone back.

"She seems good," Hannah whispered to Loren later as they watched Brooke walk up to the counter with Hank.

"I think she's doing OK. The running has been like her therapy. How is Hank?"

"I don't know. He hasn't really mentioned Jason, but I think he's working through it."

"How was your summer?" Lauren asked.

"It was fine. A little…eye-opening."

"You were working for your Dad, right?"

Hannah nodded.

"Everything OK there?" Loren asked.

"I hope so. Being away for a year put some things in perspective." Hannah looked up as Hank and Brooke returned to the table with two trays of Gutter Slop.

They stuck around for a few games of Rockin' Bowl after everyone had caught up, but the girls were ready to go by 10:30. Hank suggested going into The Shack to see who was playing – maybe get another drink – but the overwhelming opinion was that they should head back to the apartment and try to get some rest so they could "get the hell out of Racquet Club" at first light.

***

The same auburn-haired girl as last year was working the Student Orientation Services table when they arrived on campus. Once he'd gotten his room assignment, Hank stepped to the side to let Hannah, Brooke, and Loren check in. He and Braden were in the same building as last year – "Eldredge – 1178" – just one floor up.

Hannah was the first to return. She held up an envelope with "Taylor – 850" scrawled across the front.

"Looks like you'll have to put on shoes when you come calling this year," she said.

"Still a single?" Hank asked.

"It better be!"

Loren and Brooke were at the table a bit longer. When they finally turned around, it was clear that something was wrong.

"What did you get?" Hannah called over to them.

Loren held up the envelope: "Esmond – 302"

Hannah sighed.

"What's wrong?" Hank asked.

"That was Jason's building."

"Oh."

"Why don't you go on ahead?" Hannah said as she turned to join Brooke and Loren. "I'll catch up with you later."

~

"The first time is bound to be the worst," Loren said as they stepped into the dorm lobby. "After that, it can only get easier."

Brooke knew she was right. There were sure to be some shaky moments in the weeks ahead, times when unexpected reminders would ambush her when she least expected them. Walking into Jason's old building was just the first of many such challenges that she would need to overcome.

"What floor was Jason on?" Hannah asked.

"Six."

"Well that's great," Loren said. "Our dorm is on three. We don't even have to pass it."

"*Or* we could just go to his room," Hannah suggested as she hit the elevator call button.

Loren gave her a shocked look.

"You've been back to his house to visit Cathie, right?" Hannah continued. "Why not rip off the band-aid?"

"Maybe you're right," Brooke said as they stepped into the elevator. "Let's go to his room."

"Are you *sure?*" Loren asked uncertainly.

Brooke punched the button for six. "What's the worst that can happen, right?"

The doors opened on Jason's floor, which was thick with newly-arrived freshmen. Middle-aged men stood outside every other dorm room as their wives remained inside, unfolding stiff new sheets.

"Isn't it funny how everyone's mother make's their bed freshman year?" Hannah noted.

"Mine didn't," Brooke said as they slipped through the crowd.

"Mine didn't either," Loren added. "Who made *your* bed?"

"My father," Hannah replied, realizing her observation didn't apply to any of them. "Maybe we're the exceptions that prove the rule?"

No one answered.

Brooke had stopped at the doorway to Jason's old room, where a skinny kid in a Will Baker Band T-shirt was seated on the freshly made bed inside, talking to his parents. Brooke looked around the room, expecting to see the familiar band posters, but the walls were bare and white.

"Can I help you?" the boy's father asked.

Brooke smiled softly. "No. I was just looking for a friend who used to live here." Her eyes lingered on the boy a moment longer before she turned to rejoin her friends.

There was something soothing in seeing the room getting a fresh start.

"I don't know why," Brooke told Hannah and Loren. "But I do feel a little better."

Hannah smiled. *"Good."*

"What do you say we check out our room and get moved in," Loren said.

~

Braden was sitting on his bed reading a book when Hank opened the door.

"Brady, what the hell are *you* doing here?"

Braden smiled. "Good to see you too."

"When did you get here?"

"This morning."

"Why the heck didn't you call any of us?"

"I just figured I'd see you guys here. Are the girls back?"

"They are. Hannah and I got here yesterday. I don't know if you heard, but Brooke actually came back over the summer."

"*Really?*" Braden seemed genuinely surprised. "I'd have thought Grimwood would be the last place she'd want to be."

"It seems like she did OK. One strange thing though, I guess she and Loren are in Esmond Hall this year."

"Oh. Wasn't that…"

"Yeah."

"Well *that* sucks."

"Hannah went with them for moral support."

"When did Loren get back?"

"Well, it's not like she ever really left, right?"

Braden's eye narrowed. "What do you mean?"

"Oh… shit. I thought you knew. Loren was in town all summer. She stayed with what's his ass for a while, then shared a place in town with Brooke."

Braden looked down at the page in front of him.

Hank shifted into nervous chatter as he watched his friend

take in the news. "You should have seen this place they were living in. Totally disgusting."

Braden closed his book.

"You all right?" Hank asked. "I understand if you want to hurl that at me, just give me a nod so I can duck."

Braden leaned back against the wall with a resigned sigh. "You know, I should have figured as much. Is she *still* seeing Cole?"

"As far as I know."

"And how about you?"

"I promise you, Brady. I am definitely *not* seeing Cole."

Braden laughed. "I mean how was your break? How was Albany."

Hank took a deep breath. "Let's just say it's good to be back."

~

By the time she left Loren and Brooke's building, Hannah was craving the solitude of her own dorm room. She got off the elevator on the eighth floor of Taylor Hall, dragging her bags down the corridor until she reached room 850, where she slumped against the door as she dug through her pockets in search of her key. No sooner had she found it, than the door was pulled open, and she tumbled inside.

Hannah hit the floor with a *whump!* – seeing stars as she looked up to see an athletic girl with short brown hair looking down at her.

"You must be Hannah."

"Umm… Who are you? This is supposed to be a single."

"That's what *I* told them!" The girl said as she reached down to help her up. "Apparently there's some sort of room shortage for returning students."

Hannah brushed herself off and looked around in confusion. One half of the room was already well on its way to completion. A motivational poster with a group of rowers practicing at sunrise hung over the bed, which, like the desk and everything else on her side, was arranged in meticulous order. Hannah pulled out the envelope with her room assignment written on the outside. She removed a sheet of paper with the various housing requests printed out. At the bottom of the paper, where, if you asked her, she was least likely to notice it, the word "single" had been struck out, and "E. Cochran" typed beside it.

"What does *E. Cochran* mean?"

"Elissa Cochran. That's me."

She offered Hannah her hand.

"Great," Hannah said, realizing how grumpy she sounded as they shook hands. "I'm sorry, I just wasn't expecting this is all. I'm Hannah Merritt."

"I know. We actually had a class together last year."

Now Hannah was really confused. "We did? Like a liberal arts class?"

"No, structural engineering."

"So… you're in the architecture program?"

"I am. Don't worry if you don't remember me, it was a big lecture course, but you seemed pretty serious about it. It made an impression."

"That was definitely me in the Fall quarter, but I've hopefully mellowed a bit."

Elissa smiled. "Maybe a little."

Hannah wasn't sure how to handle this latest bit of information. On the one hand, Elissa's orderly ways seemed promising, but she wondered if living with another architecture student might dampen what little enthusiasm she still held for her major. Then again, maybe a little friendly competition was exactly what she needed.

"Where are you from?" Elissa asked as she helped Hannah bring her bags in.

"Chicago."

"Ah, that explains the architecture. I'm from Tacoma, Washington, the city of *destiny*."

Hannah laughed.

"What?"

"Oh, I'm sorry, I thought you were joking with the destiny thing."

Elissa smiled. "No, that really is what they call it. But they've never quite figured out what that destiny *is*. We actually do have some pretty cool stuff though. I own up to my hometown, no claiming to be from Seattle for me!"

Hannah gave the room another once over. "When did you get here again?"

"Technically, I pulled into town last night, but I didn't get the keys until first thing this morning."

"So… do you have a car?"

"I do. Roomie selling point number one. If you want to go to Wegmans, I'm your driver."

"That's good to know. My boyfriend has a car too, but he can be a real pain in the ass about it. He's the only one of my friends with his own wheels."

"Well, not anymore!"

Hannah's stomach grumbled. "Are you hungry?" she asked.

Elissa looked at her watch. "I am, but I'm supposed to meet up with some girls from the crew team in a bit. You're welcome to join us if you want."

"Thanks. I'll probably see if my boyfriend wants to get some dinner."

"What about tomorrow night?"

"Sure. My friends and I are going to Brownie's if you want to come."

"Definitely," Elissa said. "That sounds like fun."

***

Rather than heading to Cole's that night, Loren stayed at the dorm to be sure her roommate was still doing OK. For the most part, once she'd walked by Jason's old room, Brooke had been remarkably composed. She'd certainly come a long way since last spring, and she was a *totally* different person from the girl Loren had met a year earlier. Still, while she hoped it would never happen, Loren would understand if Brooke were to slide off the rails again at some point.

"Did you see what I found?" Loren asked the next morning as she was preparing to head to the bookstore for her morning shift.

Brooke rubbed her eyes in the darkness, still half asleep. "What?"

Loren flipped a switch and Brooke's lava lamp from freshman year burst to life, throwing hot pink light across the room.

Brooke squinted into the glow. "Where did you find that?"

"It ended up in one of my boxes," Loren said. "Kind of makes it feel like home though, right?"

Brooke studied the amorphous blob of goo as it stirred to life. "Yeah, I suppose it does."

"I'll see you later." Loren said as she slipped out the door.

She hadn't seen Cole in a couple of nights now, so after dinner at Brownie's, Loren was going to stay over at his place. Hopefully she'd left enough clothes at Cole's apartment to assemble an outfit for the first day of classes.

She was excited to eat dinner with the gang that night, but anxious about seeing Braden again. By now he undoubtedly knew she'd misled him last spring. She'd done it for a good reason, not wanting to upset him with the knowledge that she was staying behind – largely to spend the summer with Cole – but she did feel a little guilty about it.

Adding to the awkwardness was the fact that everyone at the R.K. Phillips Books viewed she and Braden as being attached at the hip, always assuming Loren was the easiest way to get a message to Braden.

"Hey! Just the person I was looking for," Mary Ellen said, holding up a printout as Loren arrived at the store and ducked into the upstairs office "I have Braden's work schedule if you wouldn't mind giving it to him the next time you see him."

"No problem." Loren folded the sheet of paper and slipped it in her back pocket. "I'll give it to him tonight."

"Oh, I have one more thing for you," Mary Ellen said. She pulled a book from the shelf above her desk and handed it to Loren. "A little bird told me you like her stuff. She'll be here for an event in the fall."

The cover was emblazoned with tall, deep red lettering that proclaimed: *I STAB AT THEE!* The exclamation point was a bloody knife blade, with a pool of crimson as the dot. Loren didn't need to see the author's name to know who had written it, but sure enough, there is was at the bottom: JANET RYLANDER.

"She's coming *here?*" Loren exclaimed as she ran her fingers over the embossed cover.

"That she is. You really like her stuff? I had you pegged as more of an Ann Patchett sort."

Loren crinkled her nose. "Are you kidding me? She's not some literary darling, but Rylander is a much, *much* better writer."

"Steamier sex scenes, too," Mary Ellen added. "Or so I've been told."

~

Loren got Hank and Braden's new dorm information from Hannah and stopped by their room before dinner. She was hoping to catch Braden alone, to save the others from the awkwardness of their reunion.

She knocked on the door and waited, wondering as she did, why she cared what their friends thought anyway. It wasn't as though she and Braden had ever been *together*. They were close. Or they had been at one time. But Braden had long ago made it clear that he wanted something more.

Maybe she did too.

But for all she knew, his feelings could have changed over the last few months. People moved on.

The door opened and there he was.

His smile put her at ease. "Hey."

"Hi, Braden." She gave him a hug, then pulled the work schedule from her back pocket and handed it to him. "Before I forget, this is from Mary Ellen."

He unfolded it and looked up. "And how is she doing?"

"The same as always. She said to tell you hello."

"She *did?*"

"Actually, no, I guess she didn't. I don't know why I said that."

Braden laughed. "I was going to say, that does *not* sound like Mary Ellen!"

Loren smiled and looked around awkwardly.

He motioned her inside. "We have some time before everyone gets to Brownie's. Do you want to come in?"

"That would be nice."

Braden took a seat at his desk as Loren sat on Hank's bed. She looked around, recognizing most of the décor from their previous place two floors down.

"You're in the same building. That's nice."

"Yeah. I guess."

"How was your summer?"

"It was OK. Kind of strange. Like going back to a previous life…"

Hank's mini-fridge hummed softly in the background.

"Can I come clean about something?" Loren asked.

"Of course."

"I just wanted to make sure you heard this from me."

"Look, if this is about you and-"

"It is," she interrupted. "I feel like I gave you the wrong impression that day we went to the train station."

Braden pressed his lips together.

"The thing is, I didn't go back to Durango for the summer. I stayed here. With Cole."

"I know."

"You do?"

"Hank told me."

"Oh, yeah, of course."

"To be honest, I kind of figured as much. How *is* Cole anyway?"

"He's good. The same."

Loren was once more at a loss. Braden *seemed* to be fine.

"Anything new at the store?" he asked.

She studied his expression before she responded, wondering how he really felt. "It's quieter during the summer. More customers from town and not as many students. Things are starting to get busier now though. The event schedule is picking up as the fall releases start coming in."

"I'm sure Dan likes that."

"He's definitely busy." Loren smiled. "I know he'll be glad to see you."

"Did you do much writing this summer?" Braden asked.

"Not really. I tinkered with a couple of stories. How about you?"

"I made some headway."

He seemed reluctant to get into it.

"What does *that* mean? What did you write? Is it a secret or something?"

"Well, I'm just about finished with that thing I started last year."

"The novel? That's *awesome*. How long is it now?"

"Boy, you get straight to the point, don't you?" Braden laughed. "Single-spaced it's about… 300 pages."

"Holy shit, Braden. That's *huge!*"

"There's a distinct possibility that it's absolute garbage, but now that the finish line is in sight, it's starting to feel pretty good."

"That's inspiring. It sounds like you really made the most of your summer."

"That all depends on what you consider time well spent," Braden mused. "It's sure good to be back here though."

~

It still felt like summer as Loren and Braden stepped outside. The quad was filled with students stretched out on blankets and tossing frisbees – carefree and living in the moment. The evening sky was bright. The air was humid. Just once – as they were passing Grimwood's statue on the way to Brownie's – a breeze picked up and a hint of cool air drifted over their faces.

"You know, I did see him once this summer."

"Who?" Braden asked.

"Grimwood."

Braden stopped and looked at her. "Where?"

"The Falls. At just about this time of day actually."

"Isn't that where he tossed that manuscript?"

"I think so, yeah."

"Can I ask you something?"

"What?"

"How were you feeling when it happened? Was something on your mind?"

Loren hesitated. "…I don't know. Why do you ask?"

She'd been thinking about Braden.

"I've been pondering Price's theory about flares. And wondering if there might be more to it than that."

"Like what?" Loren asked.

"I'm starting to think they flare in response to a person's mood, like… when their feelings echo an emotion from the past."

"I could see that I suppose."

She remembered exactly what she'd been feeling that day.

Regret.

~

Brownie's was the same as ever, save for the buzz in the air – a tangible charge coming off of the students, many of whom were eating there for the first time. It was a thrill that would wear off in short order, right around the time the house meatloaf made an encore appearance on the weekly menu.

Brooke wondered if there'd been this much energy in the room the first time she ate there last year. Of course, she'd probably been too self-medicated to notice, but tonight it was getting under her skin – in a good way – and for the first time in a long while, it felt as though she was living in the moment, while looking forward to tomorrow and the first day of classes.

The sight of Loren and Braden sitting together gave her an extra boost. Who ever knew where their friendship stood? But for the moment, they appeared to be enjoying one another's company.

"Nice to see you guys" Brooke said as she took a seat. "Have you been here long?"

Loren shook her head. "Just a few minutes."

Brooke slid into the booth beside her. "It's strange to see all these freshmen."

"Isn't it?" Loren said. "Last year I saw all the upper classmen eating in here and figured they had it all figured out."

"And how do you feel now?" Hank asked as he reached the table. "What are we talking about?"

"Life." Braden mused. "Wisdom."

"Ohh…" Hank looked grim. "You know what's better than wisdom?"

"What?"

"Beer."

Loren rolled her eyes. "My father would agree with you."

"On what?" Hannah asked when she and Elissa arrived.

"Nothing, hun," Hank replied. He slid over to make room for them.

"Take it from me," Brooke began. "You'll never find the answers at the bottom of a…" She lost her train of thought when she saw Elissa standing next to Hannah.

"Drink?" Elissa asked.

"Yeah," Brooke sighed. She recognized Elissa from someplace, but she couldn't put her finger on where.

"Personally, I think it depends on what you're having," Elissa said. "There's never been a problem I couldn't solve with a good cup of black coffee. Do you mind if I join you?"

"Not at all." Brooke smiled and moved over, watching Elissa's hands as she set her tray down and sat in the booth beside her.

"Everyone, this is my roommate, Elissa," Hannah said.

"Roommate?" Loren asked. "That's a surprise."

"Isn't it though," Hannah replied. "Elissa is an architecture major as well."

"Uh oh," Hank said. "You *may* be in trouble then."

"Is she competitive?" Elissa asked.

"That's *one* way of putting it"

"Would you stop?" Hannah exclaimed.

Brooke ate her meal and studied their new acquaintance's face as Braden and Loren introduced themselves. Her eyes followed the bend in Elissa's arm to the inside of her left wrist, where a small, black tattoo was etched into the tanned skin. Brooke studied the image, trying to decipher what it was. She had *definitely* seen this girl somewhere on campus before, just briefly, but she remembered feeling the same sensation then as well: Something between a shiver and a laugh.

She and Elissa were about the same height. Similar hair color. Similar builds. But while Brooke had worked herself down to a wiry runner's weight, Elissa was more muscular, with strong, toned arms and legs. She looked Brooke's way and smiled.

"And our silent friend here is Brooke," Hank said.

Brooke snapped to attention, her face growing warm as she realized she'd missed the last round of introductions.

"Nice to meet you," Brooke murmured shyly.

Elissa's eyes sparkled. "Nice to meet you, too, Brooke."

* * *

The first day of classes came as a surprising relief, a welcome return to familiar routines. Brooke's Monday schedule was light, with a lecture in the morning and another after lunch. During classes, she was able to lose herself in the subjects at hand, but as soon as she stepped out of the lecture halls and drifted through the crowds of students, her mind returned to memories of the previous year. And Jason. Only one other person passed through Brooke's thoughts during the day, and she wasn't yet sure what to make of it.

Late in the afternoon, she went back to the dorms and changed into her running gear. During the summer, she'd frequently taken detours through campus on her runs, where she'd sprint down the quarter mile and circle the quiet quads. Today, with classes back in session, her usual routes were too crowded to allow her the space she needed to be alone with her thoughts, so she stuck to the perimeter of campus, running full out 'til she reached the roundabout in front of the library, where she slowed to a walk, stretching her arms over her head as she caught her breath next to the curb and watched the crowds returning to the dorms for the evening. Somehow, through the mass of people, she recognized one person as he walked against the tide, making his way to the library's front steps.

Braden.

She considered him a friend, but the truth was that the two of them didn't really know each other all that well. Jason had always liked him, but in the group as a whole, she and Braden had never really made a connection. He seemed quiet, and a little broody at times, but she largely attributed that to things Loren had told her about Braden's background. It sounded like an upside down version of *Pippi Longstocking*: a curious, parentless boy, living alone in an old house, coming and going as he pleased.

Braden glanced her way and smiled.

"Hey there," Brooke said as she walked over to meet up with him.

Braden shielded his eyes from the sun. "How was your first day?"

"It was good. It's nice to get back to things."

"I know exactly what you mean."

A question popped into Brooke's mind, another detail Loren had shared with her, and without considering whether or not it was appropriate, she asked it.

"You had a friend who passed away, didn't you?" If Braden was caught off guard, he gave no indication. "I did," he said. The skin at the corners of his eyes crinkled. "Jeremy."

"How long did you know him?"

"My whole life. He was the closest thing I had to a brother."

They fell into a comfortable silence.

"How are you doing?" Braden asked finally.

Brooke looked down at her shoes, and kicked away a piece of gravel.

"I'm not really sure. How long does it take to get over someone?"

"I don't know if you *ever* get over someone if you really love them."

"Then how are we ever supposed to move on?"

"I'm probably the last person to be giving advice on this, but I suppose it just happens. You don't need to *forget* them to go on with your life. And if you happen to meet someone that you connect with, I'm sure the people from the past, if they loved you, would want you to find happiness. I mean… you knew Jason, doesn't that sound like him?"

Brooke looked up.

"Yeah. It does." She reached over and patted him on the shoulder. "You're pretty good at this, you know that?"

"No." Braden smiled. "I'm *really* not."

"Where are you headed? Do you have a class tonight?" "I'm done for the day." He hooked his thumb over his shoulder. "I'm just going to the library to work on some things."

"Don't push yourself too hard, Braden."

He smiled. "I was going to tell you the same thing."

~

"Was I being too loud?"

"Not for me," Hank said as he collapsed on the bed.

"I don't care about you. I mean for the other people on the floor," Hannah said.

"You were fine. That was great."

She rolled onto her back and kissed him, then she drew back suddenly. "Did you put the sock on the door?"

"Yes. Don't worry. It's not like Braden is going to be back here anytime soon. He's usually at the library so late that I'm passed out by the time he comes in."

"When did that *ever* happen? You were always at my place last year."

"It's happened. It's happened. But that's irrelevant. The sock is on the door. We're fine."

"This business of not having our own place *sucks*. God help us if your roommate ever finishes that book of his."

Hank kissed her. "If he finishes the book, I'll just convince him to write another." He kissed her again. "He's totally com-pulsive about that stuff. We can use it to our advantage."

"You think so? Cause we've got some catching up to do. I don't want to go through another stretch like that again."

"What do you mean?"

"I mean, let's not do the separate summer thing again. Ever."

"That's fine with me," Hank agreed. "But I thought everything was good when you were back home."

"It was OK. But I missed being with you."

"Me too." Hank leaned out of his bed and pulled on the refrigerator handle. "Did you want a beer?"

Hannah gave him a look and pulled back the sheets a little. "Do you want a beer or do you want to make up for lost time? If you have to think about it, I'm going back to my place."

Hank grinned and closed the refrigerator door.

~

"Did you ever take any classes with Mark Price?" Loren asked Cole as they lay in the darkness before sleep.

"Price? Nah. I've heard his name though."

"I had him for The Novel last year. I really like him."

"Is that the course you took with Braden?"

"Yeah. I'm excited for this one."

"What's the class?"

"The Short Story."

"Isn't that sort of a step down from The Novel?" Cole mumbled sleepily.

"Well, The Novel was about other authors' work. This one is about our own."

Which I should be doing more of actually. I *enjoy* writing short stories."

The words hung in the air as Loren waited for Cole's response. But it didn't come. All she heard was the deep sound of his breathing.

He'd fallen asleep.

* * *

Now *this* was more like it.

Grimwood campus was cool and quiet. Fog clung to the grass and curled its tendrils through the trees and walkways as Brooke jogged past. She inhaled the rich, humid air, deciding that from now on, she would be running in the early mornings, when she had the world to herself.

Brooke wound her way through the dorm towers, past Greek Row in the northeast corner of campus, til she reached the lake and tributary that fed The Falls. She was deep in her thoughts when she began to hear the sounds of people running and laughing in the distance. The sounds grew steadily louder as she plunged into the woods and maneuvered the pathways leading down to the water. As she got closer to the shore, she could just discern the silhouettes of a group of girls jogging toward her through the thick fog. It was the women's crew team, running at the start of their morning practice. And there at the front of the crowd, leading the charge, was Elissa.

A shiver of excitement ran up Brooke's spine as she recognized her. She wasn't sure what to make of it.

Elissa's short hair was brushed back with sweat. He cheeks were flush with exertion, but she was clearly in great shape. Her demeanor, just as it was two nights before, was happy and confident as she shouted encouragement to her teammates. Then, just as the procession was set to cross paths with Brooke – as if she *knew* she would be there – Elissa turned and greeted her with a smile.

"Good morning, Brooke."

Before Brooke could respond, Elissa turned at a fork in the trail, and the team followed behind, disappearing into the haze and taking the sounds and the excitement with them.

~

Hannah chewed the cap on her pen until the little disc in the center broke free of its plastic tethers and stuck up like a miniature auction paddle. She held the pen at an angle so she could get a look at the damage. If the item on the block was a different major, she'd have placed a bid.

The lecture hall looked as though it was built in the 70s and left untouched ever since. The seats were covered in a sickly green fabric. The carpet was a nauseating swirl of orange and black amoebas. Hannah found the atmosphere inexplicably dated and thoroughly depressing.

The professor stood at the front of the room, reading from an overhead transparency. He looked to be in his late 70s, and was dressed in a burnt umber suit with an amber tie. Hannah was beginning to wonder if *he* was the original mastermind behind the auditorium's interior design. She glanced around the room as he spoke, and noted the speed at which her fellow architecture students were jotting down everything he said. Realizing she was likely letting her thoughts wander too freely, she made a mental effort to wipe her mind clean of any doubts about her major, and set to work taking detailed notes on the lecture. She just wished the topic was something more exciting than the specifics of ADA bathroom compliance.

~

"How are classes going?"

"They're OK..." Hannah replied .

"Uh oh," her father's voice came through the phone. "Not enjoying them?"

"I guess I'm just eager to get to the stuff that made me want to study this in the first place. I know I've got to learn the boring stuff too, but I'm starting to wonder if it's *all* boring stuff."

"I think it's early to tell yet, but if you ever decide you want to try something else, you always have my support. I'm proud of you for knowing what you wanted to do all this time, but don't feel like you can't switch gears if architecture starts to make you miserable. Things change. I know that as well as anyone."

"Thanks, Dad."

"How is Hank?"

"He's good."

"Have I told you how much I like him? He reminds me of myself when I was that age."

"Yeah," Hannah replied. "I wondered if he might."

~

"Architecture just works for me for some reason," Elissa said. "I like the precision. It's the same with pen and ink drawings and rowing. You have to pay attention to little details or things go sideways."

"And buildings fall down," Hannah noted. "I always thought I was the same way. I mean, I've talked about architecture since I was a kid, but maybe I was fooling myself thinking you can set your path so early."

The two of them were seated in the usual booth at Brownie's. Hannah took a sip from her drink as Elissa looked around the room.

"There's Brooke." Elissa waved her over, then turned her attention back to Hannah. "Maybe you just need to ease up on things a little. Let me ask you something, what were your grades like in high school?"

"Straight As."

"Were you in a lot of level one classes?"

"Yeah, mostly APs."

"And did you do any sports, any extracurricular stuff?"

"Why?"

"Is that a 'no'?" Elissa asked.

Hannah shook her head. "I was just focused on academics."

"*That's* what it is. You're burned out! If I had to guess, I'd say you've spent more time thinking about your future than eighty percent of the people around you. Now that you're here, you should try to enjoy it a little."

"You think?" Hannah wasn't so sure.

"What's the worst that could happen?"

"Do you prefer single or double-spaced? I can give you a list."

"List of what?" Brooke asked as she took a seat next to Hannah.

"All the things that can go wrong if Hannah stops obsessing about her major and enjoys herself a little. I was just telling her to try taking it easy for a while."

Brooke looked from Elissa to Hannah and tried to suppress a laugh.

"Thanks a *lot!*" Hannah exclaimed.

"I'm sorry. That just struck me as funny."

"Your reputation precedes you, I see," Elissa said.

"I'm sorry, Hannah. But seriously, I do think Elissa is right. You put a *lot* of undo pressure on yourself. You need to have some fun."

Hannah looked back and forth between the two of them. "I'll…take it under advisement."

"Brooke," Elissa said. "I didn't know you were such a runner!"

"Oh, yeah. It's sort of a new thing for me."

"Well, you seem like a natural. Ever think about going out for crew?"

"Like… rowing? No, not really."

"Well, if you're ever curious, just let me know. There's still time to join the team this year, and I think you might enjoy it.

If you ever want to see what it's about, just let me know, or stop by practice on your morning run."

Brooke nodded slowly. "I'll think about it," she said, surprised as anyone to hear the words coming from her mouth.

~

"If IQs were appended with cup sizes, perhaps men would love us for our *minds!*"

Braden was working at the counter upstairs, and suffering through another appearance by Roxanne's favorite humor author, Regina Bundy, who was at the store promoting her latest collection of witless essays: *Curve BALLS!* Regina had appeared at the store at least four times in the year that Braden had worked there, and he could not for the life of him figure out what it was about her supposed comedy that her readers found so hilarious. Regina specialized in lowest common denominator, battle of the sexes humor.

"180 *Double-D?!*" Regina cackled from the back room, "Will you *marry* me?!"

Abrasive guffaws howled down the hall as Braden winced at the stack of Regina Bundy books on the counter, and wondered, not for the first time, what might happen if he swept them off the counter and into the trash.

"Don't do it," Dan said as he walked up the stairs.

"Don't do what?"

Dan nodded at the trash can. "I know what you were thinking. This lady is painful, right?"

"Excruciating."

"Maybe this will help," Dan said as he pulled two copies of a black, hardbound book out from behind his back. "Something to ease your pain."

Braden looked at the cover: A new anniversary edition of *Black Robes.*

"Fantastic!" Braden exclaimed as he ran his finger over the embossed seals on the front. Just like last year's release of *Revenant,* this edition promised several newly discovered introductions, as well as an alternate ending.

"There's a copy there for Loren too. That should make up for the great wit back there-" he bobbed his head toward the back room as Regina launched into her next knee slapper.

"OK, who in this room has had to buy a *jock strap* for your son or husband?"

"Jesus." Dan closed his eyes. "It's so, *so* bad."

"Yeah," Braden said, massaging his temples. "Even Alan Grimwood can't save me from much more of this."

* * *

Brooke started out early. The dew soaked through her shoes as she jogged the path that led to the lake. Sweat was dripping down her face by the time she emerged at the end of the trail and saw the boathouse hugging the shore. The massive barn doors were pushed open on either end of the building. Brooke slowed to a walk and took in the view as she caught her breath. Wisps of fog hovered over the smooth surface of the lake.

Elissa emerged from the boathouse, followed by a handful of her teammates. She was just beginning to stretch when she looked up and saw the newcomer arriving.

"Brooke, what brings you up this way so early?" Elissa asked.

"I was thinking about your offer, and thought I might join you guys for practice this morning. Assuming that's OK."

"Absolutely," Elissa said as she turned to introduce Brooke to her teammates. "Ladies, this is my friend Brooke. Brooke, this is Blythe, Morgan, Jen, and Kelli."

The other girls nodded their hellos and continued stretching as Elissa led Brooke on a quick tour of the building.

"There are about forty girls on the team," Elissa said as she motioned toward the interior of the boathouse. Brooke looked inside and saw around a half dozen girls working out on rowing machines. The rest were scattered around the space, taking down racing hulls and sorting gear. "Assuming we don't have an event, we work out most mornings from five thirty to eight."

"Is that seven days a week?"

"We skip Sundays. And the occasional Saturday," she added as an afterthought. "You have to have some sort of life outside of academics and crew, right?"

Brooke nodded. Something about Elissa always made her a little nervous.

"Do you have any questions?" Elissa asked.

"What's a typical workout like?"

"Well, if you like, you can stay and find out. You're a runner, right?"

"I guess you could say that," Brooke replied as she unconsciously rubbed her tired legs.

"First thing we do every day is run five miles."

Brooke sighed. "Oh good," she said, the tone of her voice betraying her fatigue.

Elissa smiled apologetically. "If I'd known you were coming down today, I'd have warned you to save your energy."

"Don't worry about it. I can tap into some reserves."

"You sure?"

Brooke looked her in the eyes and smiled. *"Absolutely."*

~

"Do you have Price for The Short Story?" Braden asked Loren.

"I do."

They were seated in The Writing Center's main auditorium, where one of the program's primary foundation courses was being held. In their sophomore year, every student took On Writing I, followed by On Writing II in the winter.

"I'm jealous you have him for another class," Braden said.

"Who do you have?" Loren asked.

"Professor Hawkins. He seems very… *intense.*"

"What does he look like?"

"Probably early sixties," Braden said. "Thinning hair, glasses, always has his shirt sleeves rolled up."

"Yep, I think I know who you're talking about."

"We've only had one session so far, but boy, if we don't get a concept right away, it feels as though we've personally disappointed him."

"That's better than indifference, right?"

"That is very true," Braden agreed.

The rows were starting to fill up. Loren motioned toward the empty lectern at the front of the room. "What do you think they teach us in On Writing I?"

"Maybe it's an intervention. One more chance to persuade us to drop out of the program and go into pre-Law."

"I'm pretty sure that's the course description for *Part Two* next quarter," Loren replied. "By the way, how is your book going?"

"Slow but steady, but it's getting closer. I'm almost afraid to even talk about it." Braden snapped his fingers and reach into his backpack. "Speaking of books, I've got something for you."

He handed her the new edition of *Black Robes*. "To complete your collection."

"Oh awesome. Thanks, Braden. "I was just looking through that new edition of *Revenant* the other night." She flipped the book over and studied that familiar photo of Alan Grimwood.

"You know… I don't want to jinx anything," Braden said. "But if I *do* eventually finish this thing I've been working on, I'd love to have you take a look at it."

"Just tell me when," Loren replied.

2.

LOREN COULD HEAR THE dry leaves quivering in the branches overhead as she walked back to the residential side. Her bag was heavy with notebooks and class materials. The burden of fresh assignments and rolling deadlines weighed heavy on her mind.

The last thing she wanted to do was to go to Cole's place. They'd made some fleeting reference to her staying over that night, but they'd never actually pinned anything down. She knew he'd be annoyed if she didn't show, but at the moment she really didn't care. She just wanted to get back to her room and relax.

Loren didn't hear so much as a peep as she unlocked the door. She assumed Brooke was either still in class, or she'd met up with the gang for an early dinner. But when she opened the door and stepped inside, she was startled to find her roommate lying on her bed, still in her coat, staring up at the ceiling.

"Oh geez," Loren exclaimed. "I didn't think you were back yet."

"I'm here." Brooke moaned. "I'm just incapable of movement."

Loren's eyes fell on the wet sneakers thrown by the door. "What happened to you? Long run?"

"Among other things," Brooke conceded. "I went to crew practice with Elissa this morning."

"You've been like this *all day?*"

"No. I've been like this for an hour."

"How was practice?"

"Let me put it this way. I ran all the way up to the boathouse, where practice began with another *long* run, followed by time on the rowing machines, followed by weight training. And then we took the boats out."

"Did you get to class?"

"Yeah, they did all that in under three hours. Afterwards, I came back here, changed, and somehow made it through my day. But around three o'clock, the most unbelievable muscle pain of my *life* set in. I stopped at Brownie's on my way back, cause I knew I wouldn't have the energy to leave again once I got here."

"Oh, so I guess you won't want to go to dinner later."

"Ugh. No. But please, help yourself." Brooke pointed to a take-out container on her desk. "It sounded good to me when I was there, but I think I'm too tired to *chew*. That, and the smell was getting to me."

"Are you sure you don't want it?"

"Believe me, it's all yours."

Loren walked over and flipped the lid open. "Szechuan chicken. Not too shabby."

Brooke just groaned.

"You sure you aren't hungry?"

"I am, just… not for that."

Loren started eating, only to realize the smells of the food were still getting to her roommate. "Did you want me to move?"

"I'm sorry, would you mind?"

Loren looked around the room and dragged her chair to the farthest corner, where she resumed eating. The first cold bite had been good, but subsequent forkfuls were delivering diminishing returns.

Brooke let out such a long, low moan that it made Loren laugh.

"So, I assume you won't be going back for another practice."

"Honestly," Brooke admitted. "I think I might."

Interesting… Loren thought to herself.

There was a gentle knock at the door.

"It's open," Brooke called.

The door swung inward, and a familiar face appeared.

"I hope I'm not interrupting anything," Cathie Pepper said.

"Cathie!" Brooke struggled to get to her feet.

"Honey, are you OK?" Cathie set her purse and two greasy take-out bags on the floor, and hurried over to help her.

"I'm fine," Brooke said as she slumped back on her bed.

"What happened to you?"

"First day of crew practice," Loren explained.

"I'm sorry to show up unannounced, but hopefully you two are settled in enough to have visitors. I didn't make the connection until I got here, but this was Jason's dorm, wasn't it?"

"It was," Brooke replied.

Cathie forced a half smile and picked up the paper bags she'd brought with her. "I don't know if you girls have eaten, but I grabbed some burgers from Brick's on the way."

Both Brooke and Loren perked up a little.

"A burger would hit the spot, actually," Brooke said.

Loren closed the lid on her cold chicken. "That does sound good."

"Excellent." Cathie set about unpacking the food. "Listen, have you done anything for your muscles since practice?"

"Not really, I just took a quick shower, then headed to class."

"Did you drink any water?"

Brooke shook her head. "Not much."

"All right, here's the deal, you two eat. I'm going to run out and pick up a few things. Some pain reliever and some Arnica crème will do wonders."

"Cathie, you don't have to do that-" Brooke said.

"Yeah, just tell *me* what to get and I can run out for it," Loren said.

"Girls, don't worry about it. It will give me a chance to flex my maternal muscles again."

That quieted them.

Brooke swallowed hard. "Thanks, Cathie."

~

Cathie looked at her watched after they'd spent a few hours catching up. "I probably ought to get going. It was great to see you girls again."

"It's always nice to see you," Brooke said as she gave her a hug.

"Thank you so much for the food," Loren said.

"Don't you two be strangers. Tell that to the rest of the gang as well. I'd love to have you all over some time."

Cathie looked as though she wanted to say more, but started for the door instead.

Brooke hugged her again.

Cathie touched a finger to her eye as she turned to leave. "And remember, use that crème. It helps!"

* * *

All these months later, Hank still missed Jason's company during late shifts at the station. Their music discussions between songs had always made the time fly.

As he poured another splash of Howard's Kahlua into his second cup of microwaved coffee, he felt a tingle in the back of his mind, alerting him to the fact that he was no longer indulging in on the job drinking in the spirit of anarchist fun, but rather to dull his senses before he went on the air.

He no longer wandered the halls during extended playlists. Mostly he just sat in the booth with the monitor turned down, working on his class assignments. When he didn't have work to do, he often caught himself staring at the empty chair across from him.

~

Hannah's evening class let out late, and though the lecture hall cleared out quickly, a few of her classmates hung around afterwards to discuss the professor's presentation. Hannah found herself wishing that Elissa was there. The idea of having a friend in one of her courses suddenly seemed appealing.

She was still feeling unusually alone as she trudged down the steps of the College of Architecture, and though she'd planned on waiting at the dorm for Hank to get back from the radio station, she suddenly felt the need to see him sooner. For someone so proud of her perceived independence, this was a curious new sensation.

Grimwood campus was dark. She didn't know if she'd ever been on the academic side quite this late. It seemed like a different place now. WGRM was in a brick wing that jutted out from the Student Union. Hannah walked around the edge of the building in a wide arc that brought her close to the president's mansion, where a faculty event appeared to be taking place. Light poured from every window, through which Hannah could see people strolling from room to room, drinks in hand as they mingled and conversed. Two men, both dressed in the stereotypical tweed sport coats of academia, strolled down the back steps, away from the glow of the mansion's windows, where they lit cigarettes in the darkness, and exhaled plumes of swirling smoke.

Probably professors from The Writing Center, Hannah thought to herself.

She watched as one of them stared up at Grimwood Library's tower. He held the building in his gaze for several moments before he turned and rejoined the other figure on the lawn.

A woman stepped out onto the porch and called to the two men. "Walter, Mark, it's your favorite part of the evening."

The silhouettes turned and muttered to one another as they headed back inside. Hannah's eyes scanned the windows to see where they might turn up next. When she couldn't find them, she pivoted on her heel and headed around the back of the Student Union toward the library. Her vision briefly slipped into blackness as she rounded the corner of the building, the glow of the mansion's lights falling away behind her. It was then that she heard a raspy inhale of air to her right, followed by an exhale to her left. Suddenly, two black figures rushed past her simultaneously, one on either side. Her head shot to the right, then to the left as she reacted to their passing. No sooner did she see them than they were gone.

Hannah stopped dead in her tracks and swallowed hard.

Hello? she mouthed into the blackness around her, but no sound came out.

Her heart was throbbing in her chest.

She knew she had seen someone. *Two* people. She was certain it hadn't been her imagination. But as she surveyed the murky expanse of lawn before her, she could see no place where two individuals could have run to so quickly.

She'd recoiled and they were there – blinked and they were gone.

Hannah held her breath, waiting as long as possible for her eyes to adjust to the darkness, then she took off in a sprint toward the radio station.

~

Hannah was sitting on the ancient couch in the station's lobby when Hank emerged from the broadcast booth.

"What are you doing here, babe?" he asked when he saw her.

She got to her feet. "I just wanted to see you."

"Is everything OK?"

"Yeah," she said, giving him a quick kiss, but pulled back at the taste of scorched coffee and Kahlua on his breath. "Have you been drinking?"

Hank's hands dropped away from her shoulders. "Just a splash. One of the station guys keeps a bottle around for the late shifts."

The speaker in the lobby crackled to life as *The Best of Howard Lester* came on the air.

Hank motioned toward the speaker. "That's him actually"

"Can I steal a nip?" Hannah asked.

"Sure." His eyes narrowed as he studied her face. "You sure you're all right?"

"Would you please stop asking me that?"

Hank grabbed a couple of paper cups from the water cooler and headed down the hall. He returned with two hefty pours of Howard's coffee liqueur, and handed one of the cups to Hannah as they took a seat on the old couch.

Hannah sipped her drink. "This is good."

"How was your day?" Hank asked.

She shrugged. "How was yours?"

"It was OK. Kind of… lonely."

"Same here." She leaned her head on his shoulder.

"Things will get better." he said.

Hannah sighed. "I think I hate my major."

"Why do you say that?"

"Because it's true."

Hank put his arm around her and pulled her close.

Howard's voice droned softly from the speakers down the hall as Hannah's thoughts flashed to the dark figures that had bolted past her just a short time ago. She considered telling Hank about them, but she wasn't sure how he would react.

"Have you ever felt that Jason was still around somehow?" she asked.

Hank exhaled. "No. I wish I did, but… no."

He finished his Kahlua, crumpled up the cup, and threw it into the waste basket beside the water cooler. Hannah licked the inside of her cup and followed suit. The crumpled wax paper ball bounced on the edge of the trash bin, hopped up into the air, and just managed to fall inside.

"Swish," Hank whispered.

For the first time that night, Hannah smiled. "Small victories," she said as they slowly got to their feet.

* * *

"One!"

The water rippled under the shell as it sliced through the water.

"Two!" the coxswain, a girl name Amanda, yelled from the far end.

A fine mist sprayed Brooke's back and arms with each stroke as the crew of eight pulled back on their oars in unison.

"THREE!"

Brooke's arms and legs screamed with each movement. In her mind, she could see the muscle fibers contracting and pulling, seizing up and tearing apart – self-destructing in order to rebuild themselves even stronger.

When they finally completed their circuit and returned to the dock, Brooke's limbs felt disembodied from the rest of her being. The girls pulled their craft from the water, flipped it over their heads, and carried it up to the boathouse as Coach Sharpe, a fifty-something woman with short gray hair and sunglasses, recapped how they had done. In her exhaustion, Brooke caught every third word, which seemed to be either "faster" or "stronger."

She started up the hill after practice, exhausted, but invigorated, a combination that was beginning to feel addictive. Elissa was talking with a pair of teammates when she left – Kim and Anna – two girls Brook hadn't met at the previous practices. Not wanting to appear needy, she'd decided to head back to the dorms on her own today, so it was a pleasant surprise when she heard someone calling after her, and turned to see Elissa running up the hill toward her with a duffel bag tucked under her arm.

"Brooke! I was afraid I'd missed you!"

"Oh, sorry. I just thought you looked busy."

"I don't know if you've heard about it yet," Elissa said as they continued walking. "But a few of the girls are having a little get together off campus tomorrow, I wanted to be sure you knew about it." She handed Brooke a sheet of paper with an address and phone number.

"Thanks," Brooke said as she read it. "Are you going?"

"Yeah. It might be a fun way for you to get to know the other girls."

"Hank is getting everyone together at Brick's for dinner tomorrow night too."

"Oh yeah? Well this doesn't start until late. What do you say we eat with everyone, then we can head to the party together?"

"I'd like that," Brooke said. "It's been ages since I've been to a party."

***

"First Brick Plate of the new year is in the books," Hank announced as he rubbed his stomach.

"Did it taste like there was a little more allspice in the sauce this time?" Braden asked.

Hannah looked at him blankly. "You're kidding, right? A paper plate full of rendered burger grease, mayonnaise-laden macaroni salad, and a ladle of spiced slop, and you're wondering if they over-seasoned the sauce?"

Braden shrugged. "It was just a question. There's no need to attack."

"I think Braden's right actually," Elissa said between bites. "The sauce definitely has a little more bite than usual."

Brooke looked from her salad to her new friend's half-finished Brick Plate. "I really don't think I could handle one of those tonight."

"Same here," Loren said as she worked on her own salad. "Just way too much grease."

"There's no such thing!" Elissa exclaimed. "You've *got* to lay down a nice layer of grease before you get your drink on."

"Yep," Braden agreed. "Trowel that stuff on like hydrogenated Crisco mortar."

"Exactly!" Elissa said. "And I like the brick analogy."

Braden shrugged. "I do what I can."

"So, Brooke and I are going to a crew party tonight if anyone is interested," Elissa announced.

"I'm supposed to meet up with Cole later," Loren replied.

"And I'm working a late shift at Red Tomato after this," Hank said.

Hannah was surprised. "You are?"

"Yeah. I'm sorry, babe. They called right as I was leaving."

"Well that sucks," Hannah said. "Braden, what are you up to? Should we make a night of it?"

"What did you have in mind?"

"I dunno. Maybe we should do something crazy-"

"Bowling?" Braden suggested.

"God no. We've done that enough times already."

"Rock-climbing?"

"Where are we going to go rock climbing?!"

"I'm just throwing out ideas."

"Well, throw out *good* ideas."

"All right…" Braden looked around the table for help. "Uh, what about roller derby?"

"You're kidding," Hannah replied. "On second thought, let's *not* do something crazy. Let's just walk back to the dorms. You do your own thing, and I'll go to sleep."

"OK then." Braden laughed and went back to work on his dinner.

"What do you and Cole have planned for tonight" Hannah asked Loren.

"Cole doesn't really like to *plan* things," Loren said. "So we don't end up doing much of anything."

"That doesn't sound like much fun," Hank said.

"It's all right. You've got to make concessions sometimes, right?"

Elissa jotted an address down on a piece of paper and dropped it in the middle of the table. "Well, if any of you change your minds and want to join us, this is where the party is happening. It should be a good time."

~

The gang dispersed at the corner of 77th and The Ave, with Elissa and Brooke heading west toward Greenwood, and Loren and Hank continuing on towards Cole's place and the Red Tomato.

"You sure you don't want to look into roller derby?" Braden asked Hannah as they crossed at the light and headed toward campus.

"Do you *really* think either one of us is cut out for roller derby?" Hannah asked.

"No. Probably not."

A full moon bathed the campus in blue light as they walked up the hill in silence. Hannah looked from the backlit library tower to the stretch of shadows between the radio station and the president's mansion.

She picked up the pace slightly as they turned onto the quarter mile. "Can I ask you something, Braden?"

"Sure."

"Do you remember last year when you guys were talking about the library and people seeing things around there?"

"Yeah. If I recall, you were fairly skeptical about all that."

"Was I? I don't know why I always have to be so *sure* about everything." Hannah muttered. "The thing is… now I'm kind of curious to know what people have experienced."

"You have questions?" Braden asked.

"I think I do."

"I seem to have become the person people ask about that kind of thing." He studied Hannah's expression from the corner of his eye. "What have you seen?"

Hannah recounted the events of the other night as they walked. She told him how quickly it happened, and how certain she was about what she'd experienced.

"That does sounds familiar," Braden said when she was done.

"So you believe me then?"

"Why wouldn't I?"

"I don't know," she said. "When I say it out loud, it sounds so bizarre. But you seem to have an open mind about things like this-"

Though he wondered why Hannah might think that, Braden didn't tell her about any of his own experiences, and he didn't bring up anything Loren had shared with him either.

"Are you sure you don't want to do anything else, maybe get some coffee at Brownie's?" Braden asked when they reach the residential side.

"I think I just want to go inside and enjoy having the room to myself tonight."

"I know the feeling," Braden admitted as they prepared to go their separate ways. "Oh, Hannah?"

She stopped and looked at him expectantly.

"If you ever see anything else, let me know."

Hannah nodded, even as she hoped Braden wouldn't mention any of this conversation to Hank.

~

The party was taking place at a non-descript, off campus house at 78th and Melrose that was shared by a half-dozen members of the girl's crew team. Brooke recognized a few of their names from practice.

The conversation on the walk over had been fairly relaxed, even with the typical butterflies that came with talking to Elissa. Overall, Brooke was feeling much more at ease around her new friend. That changed as soon as they walked in the front door and were greeted by thumping bass, dim lights, and the din of voices trying to talk over loud music. The entire scene transported Brooke back to the countless apartment parties she had endured in a self-medicated daze throughout high school.

"This is Carley!" Elissa hollered as she introduced a tall brunette with glowing blue eyes. "She's one of the girls throwing the party!"

"Nice to meet you!" Brooke shouted over the noise.

Carley smiled and said something inaudible before she continued to work the room.

Brooke surveyed the entryway. A pile of sneakers sat at the bottom of a staircase that rose up into the shadows.

"Let's get a drink!" Elissa suggested.

They made their way into the dining room, where Elissa grabbed a pair of red SOLO cups, handed one of them to Brooke, and headed for the keg. "You want a beer?!"

Brooke shook her head. "I don't drink!"

"What was that?!" Elissa asked.

"I don't-" Brooke stopped, noticing several liters of Coke lined up on the table. "Nevermind," she replied as she filled her cup with soda.

"I'd better make the rounds!" Elissa explained.

She walked over and began joking around with the guy manning the tap. A minute later, Kelli drifted over, giving the guy a long kiss before the two of them continued talking to Elissa.

Brooke was feeling increasingly out of her element. Though everyone around her seemed nice, she would never have expected to find herself at this kind of party. From what she could tell, a few of the girls were paired off in couples, the rest were there with guys who looked to be either athletes or Greeks.

So far, Elissa didn't seem to be with anyone.

Brooke turned to the living room, where the music was the loudest, and watched a group of revelers dancing in the middle of the room. She could just picture Jason out there, boogying with his backpack on. The image made her smile. When she turned back to the dining room, Elissa was gone.

Brooke crossed the room and peeked through the doorway into the kitchen. Aside from a couple making out against the refrigerator, the room was empty. She returned to the foyer, and was just debating the best way to skirt the dance floor, when she peered through the glass in the front door, and saw Elissa out on the front porch, smoking a cigarette and drinking her beer. She was talking to Morgan and Blythe, two girls Brooke *did* know from practice. She seemed to remember Morgan mentioning a boyfriend at one point, but she wasn't sure about Blythe's status.

Elissa set her hand on Blythe's shoulder and cracked a joke, throwing her head back as she laughed, and suddenly, to her complete surprise, Brooke was awash with an emotion she hadn't felt in years. Jealousy. *She* wanted to be the one standing outside with Elissa, receiving her full attention. Rather than dwell on the reason why, Brooke took her cup, walked through the middle of the dance floor, and shoved past a couple making out at the end of the couch. She sat down in the middle of the sofa – briefly alarmed at how deep she sank before the ancient springs put up a fight. Another couple came and sat down next to her. Brooke pressed her knees together, making room for another amorous duo, but from the sounds of things these newcomers were pre-paring to have it out.

"Fuck *you*, Seth!" The girl shouted as she clutched her drink.

"Well, fuck you *too*, Abigail," her date shouted back as he set his cup down on the coffee table in front of them.

In the next moment, Abigail drunkenly hurled her drink at Seth, who nimbly dodged the airborne rum and Coke as it drifted past his face and splashed all over Brooke.

Brooke struggled to get up, twice falling back into the sunken couch, before she finally got to her feet and turned to see Seth and Abigail had stopped fighting and were now violently making out.

Brooke again looked for Elissa, but she was nowhere to be seen. When she turned back around, the amorous warriors were on their feet and headed for the stairs. Brooke reclaimed her spot in the middle of the couch, where she nursed her Coke, trying to make it last. She continued to sit there, through music changes and a revolving door of couch mates and unfamiliar crew team members. Finally, when she'd finished her soda and was about ready to make a run for the exit, Brooke looked down at the table in front of her and noticed Seth's abandoned drink was still sitting there. It was filled to the rim. The surface thumped along to the music, ringlets rippling from the center of the cup outwards, as if signaling either the approach of a tyrannosaurus, or the return of Seth and Abigail.

Brooke glanced over her shoulder. The coast was clear.

If she wanted the drink it was hers for the taking.

She leaned forward, hesitated, then grabbed the cup and brought it to her nose. It smelled like Dr. Pepper. She wasn't sure what, if anything, might be mixed in. Definitely not rum. Vodka was another question. There was only one way to find out.

Before she could second-guess herself, Brooke took a deep breath, brought the drink to her lips, and chugged it down. By the third or fourth swallow, she knew that it was spiked. By the time she reached the bottom, she didn't care.

She sat back, refusing to think about what she'd just done.

Time passed, and the booze did its work. Eventually, that numb, woozy feeling settled in like an old friend. Brooke got to her feet – unsteadily but without hesitation – and wandered into the next room to fix herself another drink. The plastic vodka bottle gurgled in her hands. A splash of soda, and she was fumbling with the plastic top.

She chugged *that* drink down as well, and the night drifted on.

She'd stopped looking for Elissa, and if Elissa was looking for her, they were missing each other in the drunken crowd, listing ships passing in the night. For all Brooke knew, Elissa had added her sneakers to the growing pile in the foyer, and slipped upstairs to a darkened room with someone else.

Sometime after midnight, Brooke stopped, looked down at the cup in her hands, and decided to return to campus. She didn't remember the walk back. There were flashes of street lights, headlights glaring on The Ave, and the shadows of the trees over the quarter mile. It was all a grimy, mottled blur.

She *did* remember stumbling into Esmond Hall and staggering into the elevator, because she instinctively pressed the button for six –Jason's floor – and was instantly jolted back to the present. She hit three as the cab began its ascent, and got off on her own floor before the elevator continued upstairs to open its empty doors on the past.

Part of her was hoping Loren might have changed her mind and come back to the dorm that night. Something in her, the part that loved Jason, wanted a friend to take care of her now. Or at least, to hold her accountable. The other part was ashamed at what she had allowed herself to do.

She walked into the bathroom, slipped into one of the stalls, and forced herself to vomit up what was still in her stomach, whatever her body hadn't yet absorbed, then she lurched down the hallway to her dorm room, and passed out on her bed.

~

Tap. Tap. Tap.

Brooke opened her eyes in the dark room.

The curtains were pulled closed, but the sharp light pressing in around the edges told her it was late in the day. Probably after noon.

Tap. Tap. Tap.

Her eyes drifted toward the door. She hadn't felt like this in a *very* long time. Hung over and soaked with regret. The film on her teeth reminded her that she'd thrown up the night before, but not before much too much alcohol had seeped into her blood and flooded her system.

Tap. TAP. Tap!

Whoever was at her door was knocking with just a little more force now. The slower pace, and the force of the final sound, gave the impression they didn't think anyone was home.

Brooke looked over at Loren's bed. It hadn't been slept in. Loren had spent the night at her boyfriend's place off campus.

Bleary images from the party swam back through her vision as she got to her feet, pushed through the nausea, and went to the door. She opened it just in time to see Elissa starting down the hall.

"Wait-" Brooke called after her.

Elissa turned around. "You *are* here. I was starting to think you'd snuck off with someone at the party."

"No," Brooke mumbled as she stepped back inside. "Come on in."

The walk from the bed to the door had upset her stomach. "You OK?" Elissa asked.

"Yeah, I just need to lie back down. I'm *really* hung over."

"Oh, I'm sorry to hear that."

"You and me both," Brooke said as she slumped back on her bed.

"Is your roommate here?"

"No." Brooke shook her head. "And if you wouldn't mind, I'd rather not tell her about this."

A fresh wave of shame and *nausea* washed over her.

"Sure thing," Elissa replied. "What were you drinking last night?"

"Definitely a lot of vodka." Brooke pulled a cold hand to her forehead. "And *probably* a fair bit of gin," she continued, as she set her other hand on her stomach.

"I'm sorry. I've been there. Did you want anything to eat?" Elissa asked. "I can run to the corner store."

"I don't think I could keep anything down."

"Did you want me to leave and let you sleep?"

Brooke shook her head again. "Honestly, I'd like the company."

"I didn't know what happened to you last night," Elissa explained. "I'm sorry if I left you on your own for too long. I was talking to some of the girls outside for a while, but I kept trying to get away. When I finally did, I couldn't find you."

"I wish I could tell you what *I* was doing, but it's all sort of a blur."

"When did you leave?"

"I have no idea. I don't really remember walking back here."

"I'm glad you're OK. Like I said, I thought you might've hooked up with someone, but when I didn't hear anything from you this morning, and you didn't… turn up in anyone's room at the house, I started to get worried."

Brooke opened her eyes, the lids drooping heavily. "Sorry."

"Can you make me a promise?" Elissa asked. "If you ever get like that again, will you make sure I know about it, so I can be sure you get home safely?"

"Sure." Brooke murmured.

"You mind if I stick around for a while and play nursemaid?"

"That would be nice."

Brooke sank into the pillow and closed her eyes. She felt terrible. The shame of falling off the wagon was settling in heavy now, but the fact that Elissa had come looking for her *had* to be a good thing. It reminded her of Jason.

~

"So, what's the deal with Cole?" Hank whispered to Braden as they settled into the booth at Brownie's. "Is he a student here or what?"

Braden eyed Loren's boyfriend at the far end of the table.

"I think he's been enrolled off and on," Braden whispered back. "He seems to enroll in a program, stick around for a quarter or two, then drop out."

Hank looked across the table at Brooke, who was slumped in a chair, staring at a piece of dry toast and a mug of tea. "What's up with her?" he asked Elissa.

"She overdid it last night," Elissa replied.

Loren, overhearing the conversation, looked from Hannah to Hank, and then to Braden. Their eyes locked for a moment as they realized something had gone haywire the night before.

"What?" Elissa asked when she realized something was up. She looked at Hannah, who shook her head slightly as if to alleviate her concerns.

Brooke took a bite of toast and looked around the table without a word.

Braden broke the silence first. "Loren, have you written that paper for Gridley yet?"

"Just about," she said. "I need to put the finishing touches on it tonight. I won't even ask how yours is coming. I don't need the aggravation."

"What aggravation?" Cole asked.

"He always does the papers the day they're assigned," Loren explained. "It's obnoxious."

"You'll be happy to know I'm not actually done with this one yet," Braden replied.

"I don't believe it."

Braden held up his bag. "It's true. I'm heading to the library after this to hammer it out."

"Music to my ears," Loren said. Noticing the lightness of his bag, she added "I swear, every time I see you you're carrying less and less stuff."

"Oh yeah?"

"She's right," Hannah said. "You used to haul that massive backpack back and forth last year. Don't you have any books for your classes?"

Braden unzipped the bag and held up his poetry book and a pair of notepads.

"One textbook and the materials for your novel," Loren said. "That's all you're carrying in there?"

"That's it. What's your bag look like?"

Loren leaned over and hoisted a bulging book bag up onto the table. It landed with a *thunk*.

"That's not just for Gridley's class though, right?"

"No," Loren said. "I want to go through a bunch of stuff for Tuesday as well-"

"Tonight?" Cole interrupted. "I thought we were going to The Little after this."

"We can't tonight, baby," Loren said to him. "I'm working the Janet Rylander event tomorrow, so I need to get a head start on some things."

"Oh yeah, that's tomorrow," Braden said. "I'm on the

schedule for that one too. We'll have to compare notes after her talk."

"I think I'm working that event too actually," Cole said. "What's the book called again?"

Loren rubbed her hands together. "I Stab at Thee!"

"I Stab at Thee?" Hank asked. "Who is this author, Ricardo Montalban?

Loren looked perplexed "Who?"

"The Fantasy Island guy," Braden explained. "He played Khan in *Star Trek II.*"

At Loren's continued lack of recognition, Braden looked at Cole questioningly.

"Very few girls know sci-fi," Cole explained.

"To the last, I grapple with thee," Hank exclaimed. "From hell's heart, I stab at *thee!*"

"God, I had no idea you were such a nerd!" Hannah said.

"I'm not!"

"I think everyone gets a free pass where *Star Trek* is concerned," Cole said.

Elissa pointed to Cole. "I'm pretty sure he's right about that."

"You know, that's actually a quote from Herman Melville," Loren observed.

"The hell you say!" Hank replied indignantly.

"She's right ," Braden noted. "It's from *Moby Dick.*"

"Huh," Hank said. "Well, if I'd known that, I might have read that one in high school."

"Trust me," Braden told his roommate, "It may be blasphemy, but you didn't miss out on anything."

~

tap.........*tap*

   tap.........*tap*

   tap.........*tap*

"Do you mind?" Loren asked Cole, who was holding a pencil between his middle and index fingers, bumping the eraser end on the counter, then letting it bounce up and over in a wide arc until it bounced down on the other side of his hand.

"You're a little testy," he observed.

"I'm trying to finish this paper."

"The one Braden was working on?"

Loren looked up from her laptop. "Yeah. Why?"

Cole shrugged and pulled a bottle of chardonnay out of the refrigerator.

"Is that from the SARK event last week?"

"Yeah. No one drank any of it. You'd think a bunch of women in moomoos would like their white wine, right?"

You would actually, Loren thought.

Cole poured a tall glass for himself and crossed the room to his father's old Eames chair.

"I'm sorry if you're restless," Loren said. "But I have to get this done. I've been putting it off and putting it off so we could have some fun, but it's due tomorrow."

"Don't worry about it," Cole said, though the tone in his voice rested somewhere between annoyance and a pout.

Loren watched him for a moment as he pulled on a pair of headphones and flipped on the TV, then she returned to her work.

* * *

Cole walked past the front counter with a case of sauvignon blanc and an almost comical frown on his face. He stopped at the bottom of the stairs to catch his breath, but immediately hopped to attention again as Roxanne came down the stairs.

"What's up with him?" Braden whispered to Loren.

"Other than the fact that mystery fans always polish off the wine?" she joked.

Braden wasn't sure how to respond.

"Cole, step up the pace. That should have been set up thirty minutes ago," Roxanne grumbled, then she stormed past the counter and out the back door.

Loren waited until Roxanne was out of sight before she continued. "If I had to guess, being hounded by his mother is probably what's getting under his skin right at this moment."

Dan walked by with a stack of *"I Stab at Thee!"* hardbacks in his arms, arching his eyebrows at Loren, "She just pulled up in back."

"Who?"

"Rylander!"

"You excited?" Braden asked.

Loren picked up her copy of the book, turning it so Braden could see where she'd last placed her bookmark. She was just about to the end.

"Oh yeah. After I finished my work last night, I stayed up way too late trying to finish it. It's really good. I wish I wasn't stuck down here tonight."

Braden studied the black and white author photo on the back of the book. Janet Rylander was in her mid-sixties, with short black hair – gray at the temples – and dark, sharply slanted eyebrows. She had a serious expression on her face, but there was just the hint of a hooked smile at the corner of her mouth, a knowing expression, like she planned to eat your breakfast.

Braden's thoughts were interrupted by the jingling entry bell in the café. He and Loren turned to see Roxanne leading Janet Rylander into the store and past the main counter to the stairs. Loren's mouth fell open as she watched her favorite living author disappear up the stairs.

"Go up and watch the event," Braden said. "I can cover things down here."

"Are you sure?"

"Yeah, it's pretty slow down here. If things pick up, I'll just call Cole and ask him for help."

"Oh he'll *love* that."

Loren was still deliberating.

"Go!" Braden urged her.

"Are you sure?"

"This is what we work here for."

"OK. Thank you!"

Loren grabbed her copy of Rylander's book, gave Braden a quick hug, and hurried up the stairs. Cole was seated at the information desk, ringing out customers. He shot her a questioning look as she hurried past him on her way to the back room. The seats were packed, but she managed to find a corner with a clear view of the lectern where she wasn't blocking any customers.

The audience murmured quietly as they waited for the event to begin. Dan was up front, setting out the last of the books. He caught Loren's eye as he turned to leave, giving her an excited smile and a thumbs up as he slipped out of sight.

A hush came over the crowd as Janet Rylander entered the room like a press secretary arriving for a White House news briefing. She marched up to the lectern, slammed down a copy of *I Stab at Thee!* opened it to a section she'd marked with a red ribbon, and surveyed the room with a mischievous grin. She began reading.

"Cornelius reached out with a *glistening* tortilla chip, scooping up a heaping portion of *thick* guacamole, which he shoved down his gullet, indifferent to the *oily* green chunks accumulating at the corners of his mouth."

Rylander bellowed the passage, hitting the adjectives with an excited mix of drama and disgust that delighted the audience.

"The beaded curtain rattled behind him, and a waitress appeared to his right, delivering a *steaming* platter of charred peppers and *sizzling* steak strips. A glistening, *serrated* steak knife rested atop the container of tortillas."

She arched one eyebrow, and the audience tittered in anticipation.

"'*Gimme another Cadillac!*' he grunted. The waitress picked up his empty glass and left without a word. Cornelius reached for the knife, sawed off a chunk of *seared* meat, and lifted the cover of the tortillas. Steam rose in the cool air, fogging the lenses on his eyeglasses. The curtain clattered behind him, and footsteps approached to his side as Cornelius set the knife *back* on the plate."

A woman in the audience gasped. Rylander looked up with a smile before she continued.

"'*Where's that margarita?!*' he demanded, without looking up. A shadowy figure stepped in from the side, hovering over him, waiting for the steam to clear from Cornelius' glasses. Then, just as the fog cleared, the figure lunged in. Light glinted off the knife edge. A gloved hand covered his mouth, as the other seized the worn handle, sweeping the jagged blade toward his throat. Cornelius cried for help, but his voice was cut to a gurgle. His hands clawed at the air as the serrated blade tore into his throat and *sawed* through the tendons. Hot, dark blood burbled from his neck, pooling on the table and dripping from the edge, as Cornelius' attacker grabbed the knife and slipped out the back door."

Rylander stopped, closed the book, and looked around the room. A gentleman in a bow tie sat frozen in place, a cracker heaped high with cheese suspended midway to his mouth. He blinked and set the food back on his plate, uneaten.

The audience erupted in applause.

Roxanne walked up to the lectern, clapping her hands and smiling broadly.

"She doesn't disappoint! Right? I want to thank Ms. Rylander for coming tonight. And now, if any of you have any questions, we can open the floor up for a brief Q and A. And please, help yourself to more wine and cheese before we begin the signing. Otherwise, my son will just sneak out with it later." The audience laughed as Roxanne pressed her lips together at her non-joke.

Loren fidgeted in the back, wanting to ask a question, but too wound up with tension to do so. She wasn't feeling like much of a writer these days. Sure, she was taking courses and living the life of a Writing Center student, but it had been ages since she'd felt compelled to sit down and get something down on paper, just for the thrill of putting her ideas into words.

She recognized a few of her classmates seated in the audience. One of them, a prematurely gray guy with freckles and glasses, raised his hand and asked a question about structure, specifi- cally, whether she wrote from outlines or developed her stories organically.

"Outline! Outline! Outline!" Rylander said. "*Always* know where you're going! Writing without an outline is like mental mastur- bation. *Worse,* at least with masturbation you know the ending!"

As the laughter died down, an older gentleman – who had clearly been some type of banker or accountant before retirement – stood and asked that inevitable chestnut: *Where do you get your ideas?*

"Easy. My books are all confessions!"

That drew another wave of laughter. When the noise finally settled, Loren asked her question.

"Any advice for someone struggling to find the time to write?"

Rylander peered into the lights, holding up one hand to block the glare from her eyes. "Who asked that?"

Loren raised her hand, and Rylander stared at her. "Are you a writer?"

Loren nodded almost imperceptibly.

"I'm sorry, was that a 'yes?'"

"…Yes." Loren answered softly.

"You either are or you aren't! *You* make that decision. Then, as a writer, you *have* to write. It's not optional. You make the time. You don't wait for inspiration. You don't play Hemingway and drink in front of the keyboard. You show up. You put in the hours. And you get out of it what you put in. Don't let *anything* distract you from the thing you want to do with your life. Not bills, not jobs, and especially not… *relationships.*"

Loren was struck silent. It bothered her that her first instinct was to see if Cole was in the room.

He wasn't.

The discussion moved on, and though she wanted to get in line to have her copy of the book signed, Loren felt she better get back to work. Plus, she was wary of drawing the spotlight her way again. Once a few more audience members had asked their questions, she slipped out of the room and down the back stairs to help ring people out.

"How was it?" Braden asked her once the rush of customers had finally died down.

"It was good. She's… interesting."

"I was flipping through the book during the event," he said. "I like the way the main characters take turns narrating. It reminded me of *Dead Men Don't*."

"Oh," Loren said, caught off guard by the mention of their aborted writing project from the year before.

Before Loren could come up with something else to say, the floor was suddenly a bustle of activity as Roxanne led Janet Rylander toward the back door.

Rylander stopped in front of the counter, recognizing Loren from the event, and locking her in place with an unblinking stare.

Loren froze, unsure whether to say something, perhaps hold up a hand and wave.

Braden looked from Rylander, to Loren, and back.

"What's keeping you from writing? Is it this guy?" Rylander nodded at Braden. "Is *he* monopolizing your time?"

"It isn't me," Braden exclaimed, lifting his arms in surrender.

The corner of Rylander's mouth hooked, flashing him the vaguest hint of a smile.

"But *someone* is, am I right?" Now she had Braden locked in her gaze, but he seemed more amused than intimidated.

"You'll have to ask her that one," he said.

Rylander studied him closely. "Huh, I see how it is…" Her eyes locked on the book in Loren's hands. "Would you like me to sign that?"

"That would be great, thank you." Loren said as she handed it over.

Rylander opened the book on the counter and set to work.

Loren and Braden exchanged glances.

Roxanne watched the proceedings without comment, silent in a most uncharacteristic way.

Finally, Rylander looked over her inscription, signed her name with a flourish, and handed the book back to Loren. "Good luck," she said as she turned and walked away.

Loren rotated the book and studied the inscription.

"What did she write?" Braden asked.

"Just… something boilerplate," Loren said as she flipped the cover shut.

Braden's eyes narrowed, but he didn't press her.

Cole walked past the counter at the end of the event, an unopened bottle of sauvignon blanc in his hands. "You coming by later?" he asked Loren.

"I think I better go back to the dorm as soon as we close up. I've got to finish another paper tonight."

Cole's eyebrows pinched together. "You didn't mention that earlier-"

"It completely slipped my mind."

"Suit yourself," he said before he headed out the back door.

Braden watched from the corner of his eye as Loren picked up her copy of Rylander's book. "If you want to leave now, I can handle everything else."

"Thanks, Braden," Loren said as she stepped into the back. Before she returned the book to her bag, she cracked the cover to reread the inscription:

"Boyfriends come and go, honey.
Writing is forever.
(And murder is always an option!)
– Janet Rylander"

~

Braden's stomach growled as he locked up the store and headed down the street in search of food. He hadn't eaten dinner, and a Brick Plate was sounding pretty damn good.

He slipped into Brick's and was just about to take a seat at the back counter when he caught sight of someone seated in a nearby booth with her back to the door.

"Fancy meeting you here," he said to Loren.

She looked up in surprise. "You caught me."

"How's that paper coming?" He asked, pointing to the Rylander book she was reading.

"There is no paper," she admitted. "I hope you're not mad at me for cutting out on you."

Braden waved his hand dismissively. "You didn't cut out on anything. Mary Ellen runs all the reports in the morning. I just had to drop the cash bags in the safe and turn out the lights. Mind if I join you?"

"Of course not. Have a seat."

"So what are you doing here?" Braden asked as he sat down and stole a fry from her plate. "Why aren't you over at Cole's place?"

Loren opened her mouth to answer, but just sighed. "Can we not talk about Cole?" she asked, weariness creeping into her voice.

"Sure."

Braden raised his hand to get Betty's attention. More often than not, she was their server. Yet, despite waiting on them dozens of times, the older woman refused to express anything in the way of familiarity with any of them, except for Jason, but he'd been a special case, and a local.

"Brick Plate and a root beer," Betty repeated as she jotted down Braden's order. "You good?" she asked Loren.

"Could I get a cup of coffee?" Loren asked.

"Actually, that sounds good," Braden added. "Make that two please."

"Still want the root beer?"

"No thanks."

"Two coffees, one Brick Plate," Betty confirmed. She looked at Braden over the top of her reading glasses before she left. "Just remember, you asked for it."

Braden looked at Loren. "That was… threatening."

"You know Betty."

"So, you liked the event?"

"Yeah."

"You don't sound so enthused."

"It made me feel kind of… bad," Loren said.

"*Why?*"

"Because I'm not doing anything creative. It doesn't feel like I'm working toward anything."

"Loren, you're studying in one of the most immersive writing programs in the country."

"Yeah, I'm *studying* writing, but I'm not *doing* any. It doesn't feel like I have the bug. Like all I want to do is write stories and fashion perfect little phrases. I mean, look at you, when you're not at the library working on something for class, you're staying up until all hours writing your own stuff. You're actually *doing* it."

"Well, first of all, perfect little phrases are annoying. And second, you overestimate what I'm doing with my time."

Betty dropped off their drinks and they fell into a natural silence. Braden poured cream into his coffee and watched it swirl in his mug.

"Let me tell you something," he said finally. "Just because I'm working on stuff, that doesn't mean it's any good. I'm just trying to get some miles on the engine. And don't kid yourself, I'm not at the library all the time because I feel some primal urge to create fantastical worlds, like something out of *The NeverEnding Story*. I don't exactly have much going on outside of classes and work. You've got a personal life. That's invaluable if you're going to have something to write *about*."

"You have plenty of life experience to draw on, Braden."

"Don't be so sure."

"But you *enjoy* writing, right?"

"Within reason. I don't leap out of bed with my fingers tapping the moment I get to the keyboard. I'd be wary of any supposed writer who loses control of his faculties at the mere *idea* of sitting down at the keyboard. You know who those people end up writing for~"

"McSweeney's." Loren interjected.

"Mc-*yeah?* How'd you know that?"

Loren laughed. "Because you *hate* them."

"I do hate them, and you know why?"

"Because they're glib, and smarmy, and they ruined Nick Hornby."

"That's right." Braden looked bemused. "I've gone on this tirade before I see."

"Every time a new issue arrives, yeah."

"So yes, people who claim to love everything about the process of writing, write overly clever *bullshit*. And as a side note, McSweeney's *loves* overly clever bullshit. Therefore, they are the greatest threat against quality writing."

"You know who loves McSweeney's?"

"Who?"

"Cole."

Braden sat in silence, collecting himself. "Good thing we aren't talking about him. Right?"

"Right."

"If we were talking about him though… is he at least good to you?"

"Yeah, he is," Loren said. "I have to say, I feel kind of bad for him sometimes."

"Why is that?"

In the back of his mind, Braden couldn't help but think that it was less than ideal for someone's girlfriend to feel bad for him.

"His folks can be *hard* on him about things. I almost feel like his family has psyched him out somehow. Like he could do so much more than he does."

Braden wasn't so sure about that.

Betty came by again with his Brick Plate, and Braden paused to stir the mess of ingredients together and take a bite.

"Loren, I don't mean to be rude," he said finally," but I'm more interested in you and what *you* want to be doing. Are you at least happy?"

"Overall, yeah, I think so. I just need to make some adjustments. I don't want to write 'clever bullshit' as you say, but I'd like to start *something*. I feel like I need to make some changes if I'm ever going to do the things in my life that I want to."

"Let me know if I can help somehow," Braden said.

"It helps to just *talk* sometimes. So thank you."

Betty refilled their coffee mugs while Braden and Loren began to talk in a way they hadn't all year, catching up on things the two of them could only ever discuss with each other.

3.

SHE JUST HAD TO get started. Waking early and heading to the boathouse wasn't the problem. It was painful, but it was manageable. And most mornings she walked over with Elissa anyways, which blunted any lingering fatigue, as her new friend's energy was contagious. But once they arrived at the boathouse, got changed, and finished their warm-ups, the period between getting the shells in the water and climbing in seemed interminable. Too much time to think about what was coming and anticipate the impending fatigue. Then there was the chilled air on her bare legs. The lapping of the cold water against the hull. That part definitely wasn't for her. Despite her summer of therapeutic and compulsive running, Brooke was, at heart, a sleep late between flannel sheets kind of girl.

Once Coach Sharpe gave them the signal, Brooke and the rest of the crew climbed in and set to work on their drills. That was when the time began to fly. Once they were out in the boat, finding their rhythm and cutting through the water – legs pumping, arms rowing – practice slipped by in the blink of an eye. There was no time for hesitation, no space for second-guessing. If someone in the boat wasn't on their game, it was obvious immediately. If the boat "caught a crab," it was clear in an instant whose oar blade had gotten stuck beneath the surface and stopped the shell in its tracks. That had happened to Brooke her first time out, and if it happened to you once, you never wanted a repeat performance. Most of the girls could be cool about it, but some of them, like Blythe, could be real bitches.

Their first race of the season was this weekend. Practice was intense, but not as punishing as it might have been on a typical Friday, the reason was simple, tomorrow was the Head of the Genesee Regatta, they needed that balance between pumped-up and rested.

Blythe and Carley, who thankfully rowed in the other shell, were the primary voices holding court in the locker room as the girls showered and dressed for the day.

"Listen up ladies, I know it's Friday, but remember to take it easy tonight," Blythe said. "I don't care what kind of guilt trips your boyfriends put on you, save your energy. No drinking. No partying."

"There'll be plenty of time for that at the party tomorrow night," Carley interjected. "You know the place-"

"And we'll see everyone on the bus tomorrow morning, first thing."

Brooke – who was already showered and dressed – stared through the fog that hung in the locker room air, fiddling with her brush as she absentmindedly watched Elissa shoving clothes into her duffel. Elissa looked over suddenly and Brooke dropped her gaze, hoping she hadn't been caught.

"Are you done?" Elissa asked.

Brooke looked up blankly.

Elissa laughed and pointed to the brush in Brooke's hands. "Do you mind if I borrow that?"

"Oh sure, sorry." Brooke handed her the brush as she felt her facing growing warm.

"You look worried," Elissa said.

"I do?"

"Yeah. You nervous for tomorrow?"

"A little," Brooke admitted, watching from the corner of her eye as Elissa ran the brush through her wet hair.

"Well, I know it's easy to say, but you shouldn't be." Elissa said. "It doesn't matter if it's your first time or your fiftieth, the first race of the season sets everyone on edge. But it's no different than practice, once you're out on the water, all you can do is go for it."

"Are *you* nervous?" Brooke asked.

"Of course, but I'll tell you a secret…"

"What's that?"

"It's a hell of a lot of fun." Elissa handed the brush back to Brooke as she started for the door, "I'll see you later."

~

The grass was crunchy with frost as Hank, Hannah, and Braden made their way from the parking lot to the banks of the river. They'd been up since five that morning, stopping in Grimwood just long enough to gas up Hank's car and grab a stash of coffee and donuts for the drive up to Rochester to cheer on Brooke and Elissa in their first race of the season.

"So, Loren couldn't make it today?" Hannah asked Braden as they got close to the river.

"Nope. She asked to shuffle her schedule, but Mary Ellen shut her down before she could even finish making her request."

"But she's dating the owner's *son,*" Hank said.

"What can I say? Even Roxanne doesn't cross Mary Ellen."

"I've got to meet this Mary Ellen," Hannah mused. "She sounds like a badass. I could ask her for some pointers."

Hank looked at Braden with pleading eyes. "Please. Don't let that happen."

"You're so put upon," Hannah said as she wrapped her hands around his arm.

"So, does anyone here know how a regatta even works?" Braden asked as they stopped at the crest of the embankment looking down over the water.

Teams from about a dozen schools were scattered across the water, their various supporters and personnel setting up equipment or leading warmups.

When no one responded to his question, Braden clapped his hands together. "OK then. At least we'll all be lost together."

An older gentleman in his late-70s who was seated in front of them, turned and caught Hank's eye. "Today's race is 2,000 meters, that's approximately one and a quarter miles."

"Oh, great. Thank you." Hank said. "And how do they determine the winners?"

The old man straightened his horn-rimmed glasses and studied Hank's expression closely, clearly trying to decide if this young guy was oblivious or just stupid. "The winner is the first person to cross the finish line," he said at last. "They can pass each other, but with all the bridges and turns on this river, things could get interesting."

"There they are!" Hannah exclaimed as she caught sight of Brooke, Elissa, and the rest of the team getting into position. "There's Brooke in the…one two three… fifth seat, and Elissa is in the far back. Does that mean she's the coxswain?"

The old guy sighed heavily and turned around again to explain. "If your friend is in the back, that makes her the stroke, which means she's a very strong rower with good technique."

Hannah nodded knowingly. "Stroke, got it. So she like… steers?"

Now their spur of the moment tutor was starting to look annoyed "She sets the rhythm, and the number of strokes each minute that her teammates must follow. It's much more than just…*steering.*"

"Got it, got it," Hank said. "Thank you for the-" When he looked back, the old guy was making his way down the viewing line, shaking his head, and moving faster than any of them would have thought possible. "Geez, was it something I said?"

"I guess he didn't want to be cheering from the know-nothing section," Braden observed.

~

All Brooke could remember later was the feeling of dread before the race, followed by a detached, weightless sensation as she walked down the boardwalk after her team had come in second. Or *"lost,"* as Blythe put it.

"Hey, second or third is better than not ranking at all," Elissa argued, but she was obviously disappointed.

Brooke walked back through the race in her mind, trying to recall each step along the way, but aside from the bookend moments, the burning in her arms and legs, and the rusty taste in the back of her throat, it was all a blur.

She followed Elissa through the crowd, her eyes drifting to the shimmer of sweat glistening on the back of her neck-

"Brooke!"

Brooke turned to see Cathie Pepper emerging from the crowd.

"That was a great race," Cathie enthused. "You were neck and neck right to the end."

"Cathie, you made it!" Brooke said as she gave her a hug.

Cathie glanced over at Elissa. "I wouldn't have missed it."

"I'm glad you're here. Elissa, this is Jason's mom. Cathie, this is Elissa, I've told her a lot about you."

"Very nice to meet you, Elissa." Cathie smiled warmly. "Brooke is a terrific young lady."

"Yeah…" Elissa's eyes darted Brooke's way as she shook Cathie's hand. "I think so too."

"How's the rest of the gang doing?"

"They're good. They should actually be around here somewhere."

"Maybe I'll see them," Cathie said. "Listen, I'd love to have everyone over before the holidays. If I don't see them, would you let them know?"

"Absolutely. That would be nice."

A cheer went up from the other team members as Coach Sharpe gathered everyone together for the post-mortem.

Elissa looked over at their teammates. "We'd probably better get over there."

"I'll catch up with your afterward," Brooke said.

"Of course. Go celebrate with your friends," Cathie urged as she stepped away. "I just wanted to tell you how proud I am of you."

"Thank you so much for coming," Brooke said before they hurried away.

* * *

People were still arriving, but the atmosphere was already simmering to a near boil.

"Listen up, ladies! Listen up!" Carley shouted as she climbed to the middle of the stairs in the foyer, shaking a bottle of champagne above her head and removing the wire cage as she spoke.

"I know we didn't place where we wanted to today, but look at it this way, if we'd won, there would be nowhere to go but down. So let's use this. Learn from it. And get *mad*, so that next week, we'll finish at the top, where we know this team belongs!!" The crowd cheered, raising their glasses as Carley aimed the bottle at the chandelier hanging over everyone's heads, and popped the cork with her thumbs. A geyser of cheap champagne showered the crowd as the cork flew free and jangled the dusty crystals.

Someone in the back shouted, "Let's burn this mother *down!*"

Elissa eyed Brooke, who had somehow found herself holding a cup of champagne and was now looking down at the bubbles, debating whether to risk another tumble down the rabbit hole.

"You look so serious!" Elissa shouted over the noise. "Trust me, you don't need to worry!"

"Worry?"

"They're not *really* going to burn anything down!" Elissa laughed as she tossed her drink back.

Brooke forced a smile, raising her own cup of champagne. Then she watched as Blythe – with whom Elissa had spent a disconcerting amount of time at the previous party – came over and tapped Elissa on the shoulder, whispering in her ear.

"I'll be back in a minute, Brooke," Elissa said as she followed Blythe into the next room.

Brooke looked on as the two of them disappeared into the crowd. He stomach tingled with jealousy, catching her by surprise. Then she brought the champagne to her lips and downed it in one gulp.

Here we go again.

Brooke knew she had an obsessive, self-destructive streak. It had always been a problem. Her mind was predisposed to folding in on itself, turning a thought or concern over and over, until the initial grain of worry was long forgotten, and she could no longer think straight.

Throughout high school, and even at the start of the previous year, she'd struggled with self-doubt. She used alcohol to muzzle her thoughts, and hung out with zero-potential losers so she wouldn't feel the threat of exposure. But more than anything, her favorite method of escape came in raiding strangers' medicine cabinets. In high school, it had become second nature. It was careless, and dangerous, and ultimately, it had landed her in the hospital last year.

Four glasses of champagne later, Brooke staggered through the crowd of revelers, stumbled up the steps in the front foyer, and slumped against the wall in the upstairs hall, clumsily knocking pictures to the ground with her hands, and cracking her forehead on a doorframe as she fumbled down the corridor. Somehow, she found her way into the bathroom of…whoever's house this party was taking place at.

She slammed the door shut behind her, and stood for a moment in total blackness until her tingling fingers found and flipped the switch. Her eyes clamped shut as the light burned her pupils. In the blinding white, she felt for the lock and latched it.

Then she was in the cabinet, rifling through the bottles, knocking razors, dental floss, face creams, and anything and everything else out of the way, until she found them. The little orange bottles. They were always there. No matter the place, she'd never been let down, and the same was true tonight.

Her vision went bleary as she studied the label. The prescription was for…Carley?

That's right. This was her house.

Brooke pressed the lid open with the palms of her tingling hands. Her fingers were already going numb from the alcohol.

A dozen slick pills would top things off nicely. She scooped them into her mouth, her teeth scraping the palm of her hand. When she tried to wash them down with her champagne, she found the cup wasn't just empty. It was gone. She'd either polished it off, or dropped it somewhere along her stumbling route upstairs

She opted instead to drink mouthfuls of water directly from the faucet. Then she spun around in a sloppy 180, aiming to take a seat on the closed toilet, but missing the mark and smashing down between the bowl and the bath tub. Her ass hit the ground as her head crack back on the tile wall. She slid to the ground unconscious.

While she was on her back, dead to the world, her stomach decided it had had enough of the booze and pills and opted to send them back up.

So Brooke Winston lay unconscious on a filthy bathroom floor, vomit bubbling up from her esophagus and getting swept back into her lungs as her body fought for air.

Baby, what are you doing?

Her eyes fluttered open in drowsy slits.

Cold hands pressed the sides of her face.

She looked up again. Sweaty and lost.

And there he was…

"Jason."

He was *there*, peering down at her, as cute as ever.

Jason's mouth opened and closed.

He was telling her something.

"Don't throw it away, baby." The words echoed. A soft murmur, but the voice, the voice was unmistakably his.

Then he gently slapped her awake. One cheek. Then the other. He came closer. His eyes looking down at her – tender and caring and *worried* – as he cradled her head and tipped her onto her side.

Brooke gagged again, vomiting on the floor as she pressed her back against the tub. She lay on the grungy tile, opening and closing her eyes, slowly, painfully. When she finally looked up, Jason was gone.

Someone was pounding on the door.

"Brooke!"

She clutched the toilet lid and sat up.

"Brooke! Are you in there?"

Elissa.

Brooke crawled across the floor and flipped the lock.

The door opened, and Elissa stepped inside. She took in the scene and crouched down to pull Brooke upright. "I'll get you to the hospital."

Brooke shook her head.

The last thing she wanted was for Cathie Pepper to see her like this.

Not again.

It was bad enough her son had had to save her once, but for him to do it a second time…

"I don't need to go to the hospital," she said weakly. "I just threw it all up."

"Threw all *what* up?" Elissa asked.

"Whatever that was," Brooke answered as she nodded at the pill container on the floor.

"Why did you do that?"

Brooke looked her in the eyes, reached out with her index finger, and pressed it gently against Elissa's chest.

"Oh," Elissa sighed. She sensed there was more to the story, but this was not the time to get into it. "Let's get you home," she said as she put her friend's arm around her shoulder.

"What about Carley's bathroom?"

"Well," Elissa said as she took in the mess. "The way I see it, we can do one of two things, we can ask Carley for some towels to clean it up, which will just leave her pissed off at us *specifically*. Or we can run like hell, and let her be pissed off in a more general sense when she doesn't know who did it. Which do you prefer?"

Brooke smiled weakly. "Pissed off in a general sense…"

"Me too," Elissa said as she helped Brooke out into the hall. "Let's get the hell out of here."

~

"I'm telling you, he was right here, just as clear as day."

"Who?" Hank asked as he studied the steaming mug of coffee in Howard's hands, wondering if it was laced with Kahlua.

"Dylan, man! Have you been listening to a word I've been saying?"

"Dylan? Like *Bob* Dylan?"

"No, Biff Dylan, the legend himself. Of *course* Bob Dylan!"

They were standing in WGRM's old recording studio, the room that had caught Jason Pepper's attention a year earlier. Hank looked around, his eyes settling on the console *covered* with knobs, faders, and dozens upon dozens of illuminated gauges.

Howard pointed to one of the orange, high-backed chairs. "I came in here one Saturday morning about 22 years ago, and found him seated right in that chair, with a little hat pulled down over his eyes, just fingering the knobs a little. At first I thought he was just some weirdo who'd wandered in from The Ave, but when he turned around, and introduced himself, there was no question who it was."

"What did he say?"

"He introduced himself as 'Jack Frost' and said he'd recorded an album here about ten years before, which he'd never released, even though he thought it was the best *sounding* recording he'd ever done."

"Wait a minute, you said it was Bob Dylan!"

"Jack Frost *is* Bob Dylan, same as Bobby Zimmerman *is* Bob Dylan." Howard was sounding a bit exasperated. "Now do you want to hear this story or not?"

"Of course I want to hear it!"

"So, I of course asked why he'd never released it if he thought it sounded so good, and he said it was one of the rare occasions where the equipment wasn't shit, but in his opinion, the music was."

"Dylan?!"

"Look, that's what I said too, I mean, the guy can do no wrong, right? But according to him, he recorded a trunk album here that he has locked up somewhere, even though he claims this is the best mixing console in the world."

Hank walked over to the chair and took a seat. He ran his finger's over the console and slowly slid one of the faders up. "This isn't dusty at all. I didn't think the cleaning guys ever came in here."

"They don't," Howard said. "But I take care of this one. When you have a national treasure in your midst, you need to look after it."

"What makes it so special?"

"It's a Neve 8078. One of only three made in quite this con-figuration. All hand built, with all of the typical weak points hammered out of it. Whatever you feed into this thing, it sets it down just as clear and pretty as a glass bell."

"The Beatles, Nirvana, Fleetwood Mac, Willie Nelson, Tom Petty, Creedence, Black Sabbath… they all recorded their sig-nature albums on a Neve console."

Hank ran his hand over the controls again. He's always thought he would record the first album with Jason, but now, assuming he could find the right band, he'd have to do it on his own one day. With this equipment at his disposal, he might even pull it off.

"I'll leave you to tinker," Howard said as he left to refill his mug. "Just make sure you're back in the broadcast booth at eight."

* * *

"Take one and pass it down," Professor Leitze grumbled as he schlepped down the aisle, handing stacks of stapled packets to the students at the end of each row. "This is what separates Grimwood from the rest of the pack, ladies and gentleman. This is why you're here."

A year ago, Hannah would have lapped those words up like sweet cream, but what little academic enthusiasm she'd conjured up for her second year was quickly dissipating.

"Don't think for a second that *any* of you are ready for an assignment of this size," Leitze bellowed. "Think of this as me tying the lot of you up in a sack and tossing you in the river. If you can claw your way out and swim to shore, you just might stand a chance of making it to junior year."

Was that supposed to be inspiring? Hannah wondered as she looked down at the packet.

"This will take up the remainder of the quarter, which means you have from now until the time we leave for Thanksgiving to create a project you believe would simultaneously solve at least two of the town of Grimwood's civic problems while help-ing to put it on the map. And it needs to be something more elaborate than a homeless shelter with solar panels on the roof, trust me, I have seen that one many, *many* times before. I'm talking about two *major* problems, solved architecturally. Aim high, but make it feasible. Dazzle me folks." Leitze said as he raised his arms and wiggled his fingers in a slow, low-energy version of jazz hands.

~

"Just us?" Hank asked as he and Hannah met up with Elissa and headed into the buffet line at Brownie's. "Braden and Loren are usually wildcards, but I figured Brooke would be here."

"I was expecting her too," Elissa admitted.

"Maybe she's getting caught up on work," Hank said, but Elissa didn't look so sure.

"Have you ever had Professor Leitze?" Hannah asked Elissa when they were settled at their table.

"Fortunately, no. Do you?"

Hannah nodded. "Why do you say 'fortunately'?"

"Why are you wondering if I've had him?" Elissa countered.

"Because so far, he *sucks.*"

"Bingo. A sophomore on my floor last year warned me about him. He said the faculty call him Professor Black Ball."

"Why is that?"

"He has a reputation for pushing people out of the program," Elissa replied. "Junior year, the faculty goes through the rosters and decides if any students should be 'encouraged' to change their focus. Apparently Leitze has a history of driving students away."

"Great. He just gave us a major project for the remainder of the quarter. I guess I better knuckle down."

"Oh yeah, *'the big one.'* I've heard horror stories. That only gives you, what? Three, maybe four weeks?"

"That sounds about right."

"He cites those projects in his arguments for who should stay in the program and who should leave."

"Are you serious?!"

Elissa shrugged. "Why would I make this up?"

"Shit." Hannah took a despondent bite of her burger. "Did you get any pointers from that guy on your floor?"

"Just don't propose anything with solar panels. Leitze *hates* them."

"Yeah, he mentioned that," Hannah said as she pushed the fries to the edge of her plate. "Think you could put me in touch with this guy you know? I'd like to pick his brain before I get started on my proposal."

"I wish I could, but he dropped out last year."

"Are you kidding me?!" Hannah asked.

"Last I heard, he was working for a sheet-rocking company in Utica."

"*Fuck.*"

Hank pointed to Hannah's plate. "Are you gonna eat those fries?"

"Yes I'm gonna fucking eat them," Hannah snapped as she scooped up a greasy handful and shoved them in her mouth.

Hank watched his girlfriend binge eating fries, then turned to Elissa. "So, where the heck *is* Brooke?"

"I have been wondering the same thing," Elissa said.

4.

Hannah was actually starting to feel good about this whole thing. Inspired even. Not on quite the same level she might have felt a few years ago when flipping through coffee table books of Rem Koolhaas or Tom Kundig projects, or even when she'd drawn little dream house blueprints as a kid, but compared to her interest level for much of the last year, she was in the groove again. It was refreshing.

Her idea might seem a little out of place for a small town, but after going to the regatta and seeing the crowds the race brought in, she'd been inspired to look at what was missing in Grimwood. Two things appeared to be in short supply: jobs and a sense of community. As far as community was concerned, there were surely church and recreational organizations, but coming from Chicago, there was one thing that *instantly* came to mind when brainstorming ways to pull a city together for a mutual cause (even if that cause occasionally bordered on a holy war): Professional sports.

After selecting a location in a sorely neglected corner of town, and addressing specifics she felt would set the idea apart, Hannah had begun working on blueprints and an in depth proposal. She was feeling pretty good about it, and even though her idea called for a parking structure that she *knew* would be an ideal location for row upon row of solar panels, she'd resisted the urge to include them. She wasn't going to do anything to jeopardize her chances with Leitze or her prospects in the College of Architecture.

The only downside to all of this productivity was the fact that it was consuming every moment of her time. Hank was happy to see her so fired up again. He claimed it was inspiring him to work on his record label again. But either way, she wanted to find a way to make it up to him.

* * *

"It's nice to see you around here for a change," Brooke said as she grabbed her book bag and climbed onto her bed. She was dressed in sweats and a tank top, her hair still damp from the shower. "Are you still dating what's his face?"

"Of course I am." Loren gave her roommate a curious look. "Is it so odd to see me around *our* dorm room?"

"No. But usually when you're here it's because he's either getting on your nerves, or you need to get some work done."

Loren was quiet.

"Which one is it?" Brooke pressed.

"The second," Loren admitted. "I need to finish a paper and he's always at his apartment. It's hard to get any time alone to think."

"Either way, it's good to see you."

"Thanks," Loren said, and tried to go back to her work. She looked up again a moment later.

"What?" Brooke asked.

"What's happening with *you?*"

"Nothing much."

"I'm sorry I couldn't make it to the regatta last weekend."

"Don't worry about it. You had work. I understand."

"Are you still enjoying crew? " Loren asked.

"It's good."

"Anything new with Elissa?"

Brooke turned the page in her book. "Not that I know of."

"Are you sure?" Loren asked.

"Yeah, why?"

There was a light knock at the door.

Brooke's brow furrowed.

"She called while you were in the shower and asked if this was a good time to stop by," Loren said.

There was another knock.

"Gee, thanks for the heads up, roomie," Brooke whispered as she climbed off the bed.

"Want me to clear out?"

Brooke shook her head and pulled the door open to find Elissa standing there, hand poised in the air, ready to knock a third time.

"Elissa. What's up?"

"Hey." Elissa leaned around the doorframe. "Hi Loren."

Loren nodded hello and tried to look busy.

"Brooke, do you have a minute?"

"Sure," Brooke replied as she stepped out into the hallway, closing the door behind her. "What's up?"

The noise from a TV droned down the hall. Dorm room doors were propped open along the corridor.

"Listen, Brooke, have I done anything to upset you?" Elissa asked.

"No." Brooke's voice dropped a level. "Why?"

"I just get the feeling you've been avoiding me since the party last weekend, and I don't know why."

Brooke crossed her arms over her chest and looked up and down the hall. "I'm not avoiding you."

"Yeah, you are," Elissa said just a bit more firmly. "And all I can think is that I've either offended you somehow, or you're maybe feeling something that's making you uncomfortable."

"I'm not-" Brooke stopped. "Do we have to talk about this here?"

Elissa looked over as someone leaned out of one of the open doorways and peered their way. "I thought that might be it-"

"What?" Brooke said, trying to lower her own rising voice. "I don't know what you mean-" She stopped and led Elissa around the corner to a small alcove at the end of the hall, where she leaned against the wall and slid down to the floor.

Elissa sat down beside her.

For a while, neither one of them spoke.

"Listen, I'm not trying to put you in a funny position, or make you uncomfortable," Elissa said. "I've just been trying to get a read on what you're feeling. I think we've had different experiences, but we've been hanging out for a while now, and I just got the impression that you might…like me…"

Brooke looked away. She could feel the blood pumping in her ears. "Of course I like you. We're friends."

"Yeah… but I was thinking it might be something else."

Brooke sighed and turned back toward Elissa, as she did so, Elissa leaned forward, gently kissing Brooke on the mouth. Brooke brought her hands up to Elissa's face, pulling her closer as she kissed her back.

Eventually, they sat back and looked at each other. Brooke seemed shy. Elissa smiled, but as she watched her friend's expression, it was as if an invisible veil was lowered over her eyes.

Brooke got to her feet, mumbling apologies, and hurried down the hall to her room. Elissa stayed where she was, and tried to imagine what was going on in Brooke's head.

***

The smell of grilled meat was swirling down the street, the haze of smoke curling around the corner and luring them to the proceedings, even before the Dinosaur Bar-B-Que was anywhere in sight. Hank and Hannah were walking up ahead, as Loren, Elissa, and Braden followed close behind.

"So, *The Powwow*," Elissa mused. "Has the NAACP been alerted to this tradition? It sounds a wee bit troublesome-"

"Nah," Hank waved off the connotation. "No one's running around with tomahawks or anything. It's just music and food and people having fun."

"Exactly." Hannah agreed. "And the headdress that Phi Psi guy was wearing last year was exceptionally tasteful."

Elissa looked to Braden and Loren for confirmation

"It's actually pretty lowkey, as far as these things go," Loren reassured her. "We all came last year and had a great time."

"Yeah, in terms of annual underage Thanksgiving pre-funk events, it leans towards the classy side." Braden said. Then, with a pitchman's grin, he added, "Plus, with a college ID you get free admission and a complimentary margarita!"

"No sign of Brooke?" Loren asked Elissa. "I thought she was coming."

"I did too." Elissa replied as they rounded the corner at 77th and saw the crowd of students streaming to the event. Rockabilly music rumbled as the band on stage hit their stride. She had to shout to be heard over the commotion. "I guess it's just me and the couples tonight! Hope you don't mind!"

"Couples?" Loren instinctively looked Braden's way as her face flushed. "Cole couldn't make it, so I'm flying solo tonight as well. The only couple is Hank and Hannah-"

Elissa looked confused. Braden smiled to himself, wondering when she would realize her mistake.

"You know Braden and I aren't…dating. Right?"

"Oh. Shit! Yeah. I knew that. I've met your boyfriend! I'm sorry. It's just that I always see you guys together. And your boyfriend is never-" Elissa stopped and motioned to the two of them. "Anyway, for some reason I always think of you guys as a couple. Maybe you should date!"

"Maybe we should," Braden agreed.

Loren forced a smile, clearly waiting for this conversation to change course.

The music hit a crescendo as the band on stage wrapped their set.

"Ladies and gentlemen, a round of applause for The Fisher Kings," the emcee announced over the speakers.

The yard of revelers cheered.

Hank clapped along with the crowd as he tried to get a look at the band members filing off stage.

"They were good!" he said to Hannah.

"Anyone want a drink?" Loren asked.

"Yes!" Hannah exclaimed as she turned and took Loren and Elissa by the arms and led them to the bar. "Ladies, I'm allowed dinner and one drink's worth of fun before I head back to the dorms to resume work on my project."

"How is that going?" Loren asked as they left the boys behind.

"Elissa?" Hannah said to her roommate. "How would *you* say it's going?"

"She's kicking ass," Elissa said. "It's very impressive."

"That's great," Loren said. "So you're enjoying it?"

Hannah nodded. "For the first time in a *long* time, I am."

Hank and Braden grabbed trays and slipped into the line for food.

"So, no Cole again I see." Hank observed as the folks behind the service tables loaded their plates up with ribs and chili.

"Nope."

"What was Elissa saying to you guys?"

"She was just confused," Braden said.

"What do you think Loren thought?" Hank asked as he ladled a scoop of beans over his food.

"She didn't seem so amused," Braden admitted.

"Ever think you guys *should* be dating?"

Braden stopped and looked him in the eye. "Of course I do, but you've seen how it goes when I bring that up, it's like flipping the self-destruct switch on our friendship-"

Hank studied his friend's expression. "Why *is* she with Cole?" he asked. "I still haven't gotten an answer on that one."

"I really don't know," Braden muttered as the next band began to plan. "But this conversation can only lead to trouble."

~

Alcohol, administered in the right proportions, can work wonders. Unfortunately, like mercury, it's a spiritual switch with a hair trigger temperament. One wrong move, and something is bound to blow up in your face.

For most of the evening, the gang struck a happy balance. They ate. Hank and Hannah shared a few dances on the dirt-yard dance floor, then Hannah ambled happily on her way back to campus, and Hank and Elissa teamed up for a trip to the bar for a fresh round of margaritas.

Braden's teeth felt… *tingly*. If past experience was any measure, he should have known it was time to call it quits, but numb incisors go hand in hand with lowered inhibitions, a phenomenon even the most diehard of introverts can appreciate. Instead of keeping a safe distance, he tapped Loren on the shoulder and bobbed his head toward the dance floor. She flashed an uneasy smile, but went along with it. Two songs later, they were still dancing in the thick of the crowd and having a great time. Across the yard, through the upraised hands of their fellow revelers, Braden saw Hank watching them, a tray of margaritas in his hand; their eyes met, and his roommate gave him an encouraging nod.

Braden's stomach tensed as he watched Elissa and Hank walk over and take a seat atop a concrete wall at the edge of the yard.

"It looks like they got us another round," Braden hollered over the music.

Loren brushed her hair behind her ear. "I guess we ought to head back."

"You guys were looking good out there," Elissa said once Braden and Loren had made their way back through the crowd.

"That was fun!" Loren said.

Hank handed them their drinks "You kind of have some moves, Braden!"

"Thanks, I think."

The four of them clinked their glasses together, though Hank and Elissa had already made sizeable dents in their beverages.

Hank exhaled like a pitchman in a Coke commercial and pointed his thumb over his shoulder. "Elissa, care to cut a rug?"

"Why the hell not?" Elissa polished off the rest of her margarita and hopped down off the wall.

Loren and Braden sipped their drinks and watched their friends slip into the crowd.

"Can you believe it's almost Thanksgiving?" Braden asked.

"The year is going fast."

"Are you having a good one?"

"Eh, it's been OK. How about you?"

"About the same I'd say."

"Are you working on anything, outside of assignments?" Loren asked.

"Yeah, I'm still tinkering. You?"

Loren shook her head. "I want to, but I just haven't found the time… Do you remember *'our baby?'*"

"*'Dead Men Don't?'* Of course I do."

"I feel really bad about how that ended."

Braden studied the lime wedge in his glass. "Yeah me too."

"I think it could have been good. I shouldn't have trashed it. I'm sorry."

"Me too…"

At some point, he wasn't sure when, Braden put his arm around her, and Loren gently leaned her head against his chest.

He hoped his heartbeat wouldn't scare her away.

~

"Where is everybody headed?" Hank asked at the end of the night.

The sky was black and the crowd was dissipating as the event staff began taking down the tables and cleaning up.

"I'm going back to campus," Elissa replied.

"Me too." Hank turned at Braden and Loren. "What about you guys?"

"I'm supposed to go to Cole's," Loren said.

Hank could *see* Braden's shoulders drop slightly.

"It's getting pretty late," Braden said. "I'll walk you up there."

"Thanks," Loren said quietly. "What did you think of The Powwow?" she asked Elissa.

"That was a lot of fun. The name is still a sticky wicket, but I'll definitely be back next year."

"Sticky wicket?" Hank asked as he and Elissa started toward The Ave.

Elissa just laughed.

Braden and Loren started up Greenwood Avenue, past windows flickering with the blue light of late night television. Fallen leaves crunched underfoot as they walked along the shadowy sidewalk.

"That was a fun night," Loren said after a time. "We should do that again."

Braden was quiet.

They walked further.

"Are you OK?" she asked.

"Yeah, I'm fine," he murmured.

Shit. Loren thought to herself. *She knew this had been a mistake.*

"Maybe I can talk Cole into coming out with us next time."

"Maybe so-"

They continued on, Braden looking down at his feet, Loren watching him uneasily from the corner of his eye.

"This is it," she said when they reached the walkway in front of Cole's building. "Be careful going back to campus, Braden."

Braden exhaled heavily. "Do you have to go in there?"

"What?"

"The guy wouldn't even hang out with you tonight. He could have come out, he just never wants to do anything with your friends." Braden caught his breath and continued. "Didn't we have a good time? If anything, we should be walking back to the dorms *together*. I shouldn't be walking you to *Cole's* place to make sure you get back safely."

"Braden, can we just call it a night? It was a *great* night. Let's not ruin it."

"Then don't go up there to him. He's a jerk. You know it. I *know* you know it."

"He's not a jerk. You don't even know him."

"Yeah, I do. And I don't get why you're wasting your time-"

"Braden. *Stop!* Things are finally good with us again. Why are you doing this now?"

He looked down at the ground again, kicking the leaves to either side of his feet. "Because… I love you," he said. "Don't you get that?"

Loren stared back at him, but she didn't know what to say.

"I'm in love with you," Braden said again. "Don't you have any of the same feelings?"

"I'm sorry, Braden. I don't."

Loren studied his downturned face, trying to meet his gaze, but when he didn't look up, she turned and started up the walkway.

Braden watched from the sidewalk as she fished her keys from her pocket and let herself in without looking back.

Braden stood in the darkness.

Then he started back to campus alone.

5.

"I DON'T UNDERSTAND WHAT I'm looking at here," Professor Leitze said, rubbing his chin as he stood over Hannah's plans

Hannah opened her mouth to speak, but her mind had gone to static, the white noise of a blank tape. That day's class, the session the entire quarter had been leading up to, was taking place in a large conference room in the College of Architecture. Tables were pressed against the walls, with blueprints, models, and presentation materials for the proposed projects spread out at each students' designated location. Written materials had been turned in the night before so Leitze would have time to read them over.

Hannah and her peers circled the room for the first hour, seeing what everyone had come up with. There were plans for light rail stations, community centers, shopping plazas, and office parks. There was definitely some impressive work on display, but nothing that made Hannah feel insecure about her arena proposal. She walked the room like everyone else, exchanging pleasantries and asking the occasional question. All the while, she studied Leitze to gauge his reactions. He kept his cards close to his chest, but for the most part, their professor seemed satisfied with what he was seeing. On a few occasions he even smiled and nodded as his inquiries were answered to his satisfaction. Then he'd headed to Hannah's table, with a flat glint in his eyes that made her nervous.

"This is something you think would complement *Grimwood?*" Leitze asked. "Take me through your logic."

Hannah cleared her throat. "Well, I'm from Chicago, and-"

"Grimwood is not Chicago."

Her blood pressure surged.

"I know that," Hannah replied, "but something I grew up with that I felt would be a great addition to Grimwood is some professional sports teams. Chicago-"

"Is a major metropolitan city, Ms. Merritt," Leitze interjected. "Grimwood is very different. What types of franchises do you imagine playing in your arena in *this* market?"

Now she was feeling backed into a corner. "The usual things," Hannah said defensively. "Hockey, basketball-"

"*Here?*" Leitze laughed. "Hockey *maybe*, but you think the NBA is going to extend a franchise to *Grimwood?!* They won't even give *Seattle* a new team. This is basic research."

He shot her proposal a final, perfunctory glance, and continued on, leaving Hannah shell shocked in his wake. She looked around, but none of her classmates would meet her gaze. Her face burned as her eyes teared up.

No one else was called on the mats in a similar manner.

A short time later, they broke for lunch.

On her way out of the building that evening, Hannah was surprised to see a rolled up copy of her proposal sitting in her department mailbox. She unrolled it slowly, wary of what she would find. Leitze's final comment was scrawled out in black ink at the top of the page:

D+

See me with questions.

She rolled up the thick proposal and, in one smooth motion, pitched it in the trash as she walked out the door.

There was no way in hell she was going to that asshole for an explanation. Whatever his reasons might be, she rejected them flat out.

~

"What's the matter with you?"

"What do you mean *'what's the matter with me?'*" Hannah snapped.

She and Hank were lying in the shadows in his dorm room, where, for most of the evening, she had been brushing off his every advance.

"Do you want to get something to eat," Hank asked, his thoughts shifting to another favorite activity.

"I don't know…"

"Well, you don't seem interested in anything else I have to offer."

"Won't Braden be back soon?"

"I doubt it."

"Where is he?" Hannah asked.

"The bookstore? The library? Who knows?"

Hank leaned over, brushing her hair from her forehead.

She sighed. "I'm not all that hungry."

"OK then. No food. No sex. Do you want a beer, or should we just stick a stake in this Friday?"

"*Now* you're just making me feel bad," she muttered, her tone again growing sharp.

"You've been miserable since the moment you got here. What is wrong?"

"Oh, I'm sorry, are my emotions keeping you from getting off?"

Hank cocked his head, annoyed. "Yes. Because that's *exactly* what I was implying, Hannah."

"How should I know what you're implying? I'm not a god-damn mind reader."

"No, you just know what's best for anyone and everyone around you!"

"Is that *right?*"

"Hold on." Hank raised his hands. "Why don't we take this down a notch? Instead of picking a fight, would you please just tell me what is the matter?"

Hannah wavered. Her initial instinct was to continue ramping things up, to use drama as an escape hatch to avoid discussing what was really eating at her. But for once she was with someone she didn't want to risk driving away, and she wasn't sure Hank would put up with it.

"My project bombed."

"Which project? The one you've been working on *all quarter?*"

She nodded.

"You just turned it in! How could it have bombed?"

"I don't know. But it did. I might as well be out of the program at this point. Leitze has a reputation for cutting people, and he hated everything about my proposal. I feel like I've been deluding myself."

"When did you turn it in?"

"Today."

"*Today?!*" Hank shouted, incredulous. "And he already handed out your grades?"

"Yep."

"What did you get?"

"A D+"

"Did he give everyone their scores?"

"I assume so."

"That's not right. You can't spend an entire quarter on something, and have your professor torpedo it in an afternoon." Hank shook his head. *"Fuck that guy.* At this stage, someone like that should be working to inspire his students, not knock them down. If it were me, I'd complain. It doesn't sound like he gave you a fair shot."

"Yeah," she muttered. "Maybe you're right. I'm just trying to decide."

"Decide what?"

"If I even care at this point."

"What do you mean? You've been wanting to do this since you were a kid. Hasn't architecture always been your dream?"

"Yeah, but maybe dreams fade."

***

The third week of November felt like a pivot point. The temperature plunged, classes wrapped for Fall quarter, and everyone shifted into a winter mindset.

Although Hannah closed out her course with Leitze with decidedly low marks, there was no discussion of her future in the program. She seemed all but invisible in the College of Architecture, but she was still there, hanging on by her fingernails.

For everyone else, the end of the quarter, and the conclusion of finals felt more routine. They studied. They met for meals. They took their exams. And they celebrated in their own personal ways.

Crew season transitioned to a sleepy mid-winter lull, which Brooke found disorienting. Though they had no more events on the calendar, most of the team still met up several times a week to go for a run and workout in the boat house. She'd been keeping her distance from Elissa ever since that kiss in the hall. Neither of them had spoken about it or made a move to repeat it since, but Brooke thought about it often.

Braden and Loren continued in their separate orbits, remaining courteously friendly, but mutually cautious; important, since the store was entering the holiday shopping season and they were frequently scheduled to work together, often alongside Cole. Braden found himself watching the two of them at work occasionally, wondering what, if anything, Loren had told Cole about the friction between them. Most of the time, he was confident she'd said nothing, but there were moments when he was sure Cole Phillips was on to him.

Thanksgiving snuck up on everyone. It wasn't until an invite arrived from Cathie Pepper that they realized none of them had made plans. Hank was especially apprehensive of spending the holiday at his late friend's home. Hannah, though she was in a funk, pushed him to go.

Brooke's feelings were even more complicated. While she still felt knots of sorrow over Jason's loss, there was something comforting about having a familiar place to retreat to. She was also relieved to have an excuse for not spending Thanksgiving with the girls from the crew team.

The only one who wouldn't be there was Loren, who, at the last minute, had been invited to Thanksgiving at the Phillips house.

~

"What happens when the plows come in the winter?" Loren asked Cole as he pulled up to the house. The pea-stones covering the long driveway were pinging against the bottom of the car.

"What do you mean?"

"I've always wondered that about this kind of driveway, don't all the rocks get screwed up when it snows?"

"I guess they do end up in piles along the edge of the lawn when everything melts. I never thought about it." Cole snapped his fingers. "Yeah, Manuel shovels them into a wheelbarrow and scatters them again in the spring. First time I've made the connection."

"It seems kind of silly. Why not pave it?"

Cole gave her a funny look before he climbed out. "Because everyone we *know* has a gravel driveway."

Roxanne and Keith Phillips lived in a massive brick home in the hills of old Grimwood. Though she'd built the bookstore into a nationally renowned, must-stop location for authors and literary figures, Roxanne had amassed her wealth as one of the top corporate accountants in the city. Nowadays, in addition to running the bookstore, she sat on several corporate boards, all of which – in exchange for attendance at a handful of quarterly meetings –compensated her with generous cash and stock options.

Keith Phillips came from old money. In addition to his share of a sauerkraut fortune his parents had quadrupled by selling their brand to Vlasic in the '70s, he worked in commercial real estate. But mostly, as far as Loren could tell from Cole's stories, Keith Phillip played golf at the Grimwood Country Club. In the winter months, he regularly flew down to Palm Beach and played golf there.

Something about the dynamics between Roxanne and Keith reminded Loren of her own parents. Their personalities and their dispositions echoed those of Rick and Mary Beth Austin. The serious, driven executive mother. The free spirited, slightly irresponsible father. The differences were that Cole's parents maneuvered a world of vastly higher income brackets, and they appeared to still be in love with one another. Just as with her own parents, Loren found Cole's father to be the more relatable of the two.

"Hey, they're here," Keith Phillips said as he topped off his martini.

Several people from the catering company were scattered around the kitchen. They looked up as Cole and Loren slipped in the back door, but continued working.

"Hey Dad." Cole gave his father a hug.

"Your mother is in the living room entertaining the guests." Keith said as Cole continued through the kitchen. Keith paused to take a sip from his very full glass, then he reached over and patted Loren on the shoulder. "Happy Thanksgiving, Loren."

"Happy thanksgiving," Loren said as she snuck a peak through the cracked kitchen door. "I didn't realize there was going to be such a big group here. I would have gotten more dressed up."

"You look just fine," Keith reassured her. "There's *always* a big group here. Bankers, board members, business associates, occasionally even a relative or two. Why don't we head in and I'll introduce you to everyone?"

"That would be great," Loren said, but in her mind, she wasn't so sure.

Things in the living room were bustling. Men and women in elaborate garb stood in groups, chatting and laughing politely as they sipped wine and scanned the room, calculating who they should talk to next.

A rail-thin older woman in a shimmering beaded dress stood just to the side of the front door, studying a minute slice of melba toast topped with salmon and a sprinkling of capers.

"Alexis, how are you?" Keith asked the woman.

"Oh, Keith," she said as she clutched at his arm. "I was just wondering if I dare indulge in this."

"You only live once. I say *go for it!*" Keith said with a smile as his eyes flicked ever so quickly in Loren's direction. "Have you met Cole's friend Loren?"

Alexis kept one eye on her hors d'oeuvre, but extended a limp hand. "Charmed."

"Nice to meet you." Loren said as she shook her hand. It was like squeezing a cold fish. She tried to think of something to add, but realized Alexis was already looking for someone else to talk to.

"She'll be holding that cracker for the next forty minutes," Keith whispered as they continued on.

They wove in and out of the crowd, until slowly, inevitably, they were drawn to the center of the room, the star around which the event unquestionably orbited: Roxanne. She was dressed precisely and impeccably as always. The jokes and the knowing nods suggested the topic at hand was a corporate affair.

"We'll have to see how it pencils out for the fourth quarter, but at this point, I wouldn't go booking any charters to Bermuda before April 15th," Roxanne murmured as everyone erupted in laughter.

Loren slipped away and joined Cole, who was standing off to the side of the group, smiling awkwardly. Roxanne glanced over, watching Loren with clear eyes. Loren met her gaze and nodded. Roxanne nodded back, her mouth held in a fixed smile.

~

Loren had always felt that Cole's mother liked her, but the rest of the evening played out in a strangely standoffish fashion. Roxanne was friendly enough, but every time Loren looked her way, she had the distinct sense Roxanne had just been watching her to see how she handled herself. As the evening progressed, and they transitioned from cocktail hour, to dinner, to pumpkin pie, Loren could never shake the sense that she was under the microscope, and that she wasn't necessarily measuring up.

She watched Cole, who seemed to have assumed a second skin from the moment they arrived. If he was frequently distant and self-contained on his own turf, he was forcing himself to be the opposite at this event, and the effort seemed, at least in Loren's eyes, to be quite obvious. She didn't necessarily like it, but if *she* was feeling the pressure tonight, she couldn't imagine what that kind of expectation, real or imagined, did to a person over the course of a lifetime. She watched Cole's expression, and thought she detected a hint of panic at the corners of his eyes. Then he looked her way and smiled awkwardly.

In that instant, as she had many times before, Loren felt a wave of unexpected sympathy for Cole Phillips. Growing up in this world could not have been easy for him.

~

It was out of character, but Hannah downed two bottles of Genesee from Hank's fridge while they waited for Braden and Brooke to arrive so they could all head over to Cathie Pepper's house together. It wasn't unheard of for her to have a drink now and then, but two beers so close together, when no one else was partaking, that was unusual. It made Hank a bit uneasy. Things between them had been unusually tense lately, but he was hoping the end of the quarter, and the completion of Leitze's course might help them get back on track.

For the time being at least, the beer was bringing out the bubbly and flirty Hannah, which was certainly preferable to the prickly girl he'd been living with for the last few weeks.

The second bottle clinked in the bin by the door as Hannah pulled on her coat.

"Let's get some fresh air!" she exclaimed.

"It's freezing out there," Hank said. "They'll be here any minute. What's the hurry?"

"I'm impatient."

"So what else is new?"

Hannah took a deep breath – ready with a retort – but she was interrupted by Braden and Brooke as they came down the hall.

"You guys ready for this?" Braden asked.

"As ready as we'll ever be," Hank replied.

"Do you think she'll have wine?" Hannah asked Brooke on the way to the elevator.

Hank gave Braden a look, but neither of them said anything. Braden was well aware of the recent unease.

~

"Did you ever go to Jason's place?" Brooke asked Hank on the walk over.

"Yeah, a couple times last year."

"Have you been there since…?"

Hank shook his head. "I haven't. Have you?"

"I went a couple of times over the summer. The first time I didn't know what to expect, but it's actually strangely comforting to be there. Cathie makes you feel right at home."

Hannah was laughing as she and Braden walked a short distance behind. When Hank looked back, his roommate met his gaze with a shrug and a reassuring smile. *So far, so good.*

The house looked as inviting as ever when they rounded the corner. The front lamp was on. The door open. Warm light glowed from the windows. But something struck Brooke immediately.

"There are no Christmas lights."

"What was that?" Hank asked.

"Nothing," Brooke murmured. "I was remembering something."

Jason had told her that his mother always put up the first string of lights on the day after Halloween.

"Is this it?" Hannah asked when she and Braden caught up to them.

"This is it," Hank confirmed.

They headed up the steps to the front porch.

Though the front door was open, they were all hesitant to go right in. Instead, they knocked on the storm door a couple of times and waited for Cathie to answer. When she still failed to appear, Brooke cautiously opened the front door and called inside.

"Cathie?" She looked back at the others and called again, louder *"Cathie?"*

A clattering came from the kitchen, then Cathie Pepper came around the corner, arms wide, happy to see them.

For the umpteenth time that night, Braden and Hank exchanged looks.

"Happy Thanksgiving everyone," Cathie said, waving them in. "There's wine and drinks in the kitchen. Please, make yourselves at home."

"Do you need any help?" Brooke offered.

"I think I'm in pretty good shape, but I'd love the company."

The air was filled with the smell of roasting turkey. Just as she did at the hospital, Cathie clearly ran a tight ship in the kitchen. Pots of potatoes and sides were spread neatly on the stove, the burners set just so to keep things warm.

Cathie looked around the group. "You're all old enough to drink wine, right?"

The half-beat pause said everything.

"*Absolutely,*" Hannah chimed in.

~

As they sat around the table after dinner, it was clear that everyone was thinking about Jason, but no one knew if or *how* they should bring him up. Eventually, Cathie Pepper broke the silence.

"Thank you all for coming. It really means a lot. In his short time at Grimwood, Jason obviously made some very good friends. I miss him. But I know you all do as well. Which, in a funny way…" she paused as her emotions caught up to her. "Really helps. So please, don't worry about me. I can get sad, but I *always* like to talk about him and hear your stories. And it's important to me to try and keep in touch with all of you. To hear what you're studying." She looked at Brooke and smiled. "And what new and exciting people are entering your lives."

The fire crackled.

Brooke raised her glass of Diet Coke. "To Jason," she said.

"To Jason," Cathie echoed as the five of them clinked their glasses together. "Now, as my son would say, *'Who wants dessert?'*"

~

As she'd done so many times before, Brooke studied the familiar pictures in the upstairs hallway. But this time she noticed a few gaps. Some of the more recent photos were missing. She wondered if Cathie had placed them somewhere she could see them more often, or if she'd tucked them out of sight for a while.

Brooke slipped into the bathroom at the end of the hall, the one that adjoined Jason's room. Like so many things at Cathie's house, it was strange to retrace her steps from a period that was beginning to feel like another lifetime. Her heart didn't ache in quite the same way it used to. It was almost like being in Jason's space was a comfort to her now. A kind of safe harbor.

She dried her hands and absentmindedly opened the medicine cabinet. Old habits died hard. Only now, she was confident her days of scrounging for pills were behind her. She just liked to look. The cabinet was strikingly empty, save for a handful of items which she recognized immediately.

Jason's razor, the last blade still in the handle. Traces of white shaving soap in the grip. Brooke picked it up gently and turned it over in her hands. Under the light, between its two blades, were a scattering of whiskers. She set the razor back on the shelf and glanced at the bottle of Colgate shave cream. The label was already starting to look retro. The only other item was a bar of deodorant. Mennen. That gave her pause. She closed her eyes, lifted the green cap, and took a deep whiff. The smell took her back.

The hairs on his neck.

The smell of his skin.

Jason.

She replaced the cap, returned everything to its place, and shut the cabinet door.

Her eyes went to the door to Jason's room. She briefly considered stepping inside, completely immersing herself in *him*, but she didn't think it would be such a good idea. Instead, she slipped out into the hall and made her way back downstairs.

~

Cathie Pepper sat at the end of the table and sipped her wine.

She watched Brooke after she returned. She *seemed* to be doing OK. It was funny the way feelings came in unexpected waves. She suspected it was the same for Brooke. And judging from her expression when she returned to the table, a wave had crashed over her in the time she'd been gone.

Hank and Hannah, who had seemed to be ever so slightly at odds upon their arrival, had drunk some wine and warmed to each other's company. Hannah was leaning on his shoulder, rubbing her hand on his back. It was nice to see a couple in love.

Braden smiled and made conversation, but she'd never really gotten a read on him. He seemed like a nice young man, but reserved, slightly uncomfortable in his own skin. Still, it was clear he was one of the good ones, and Loren hadn't come this time. There was undoubtedly a connection.

Then there was Brooke. Cathie looked over at her son's one time girlfriend, and wondered…

~

"Have you met anyone interesting this year?" Cathie asked.

The others were checking out the house, while Cathie and Brooke cleaned the kitchen and caught up.

"Interesting how?" Brooke asked as she slipped plates into the dishwasher.

"It's been some time since Jason. I would understand if you were ready to… move on-"

Brooke looked up. "I don't know that I *want* to move on."

"I don't mean forget him. I just mean-" Cathie stopped herself. "Look, I guess I'm one to talk. I haven't had a serious relationship since Jason's father. But you're a beautiful, amazing young woman, I don't want you to put anything off out of some sense of obligation to my son. And I know Jason wouldn't want that either."

"Well, thank you for saying that. To be honest, I don't know if I'm ready, but it's been in the back of my mind."

"What about Braden?" Cathie exclaimed.

Brooke grinned. "What about him?"

"He seems like a nice guy. And he's cute-"

"He's also head over heels for Loren," Brooke said. "I'm sure you've picked up on that."

"Yeah, I suppose I have. But she's seeing someone else, right?"

"I don't think it matters. He's got it bad."

"That's too bad, it seems like the perfect answer. Do you have someone else in mind?"

Brooke laughed. "Boy, you really want to get me hooked up, don't you?"

"It's not like that. I just want you to be happy."

"I'm OK for now." Brooke briefly considered telling Cathie about Elissa, but held off. "If something changes, I promise, I'll let you know. Now…can I ask you something?"

"Of course."

"Why haven't you put up lights yet?"

"The Christmas lights?" Cathie sighed. "I hadn't even thought of it. I guess I'm a little out of the spirit this year."

That was understandable.

"If you want any help, just let me know," Brooke said.

6.

"WOULD YOU LIKE THAT giftwrapped?" Mary Ellen asked as she handed a credit card back to an older woman in a bright red stocking cap.

"Oh, do you wrap?" The woman asked, a delighted smile flashing across her face.

"No." Mary Ellen growled. "I'm just asking you for my health."

Loren stepped in and took the books from Mary Ellen's hands. "We'd be happy to wrap them for you, ma'am."

The older woman looked shocked, but nodded her head slowly.

"Why don't you take a little break?" Loren whispered to Mary Ellen, catching Braden's eye as she headed into the back room.

"She'll be right back with those ma'am," Braden assured the woman as Loren slipped past him to the wrapping station.

Mary Ellen jammed a cigarette in the corner of her mouth and headed for the back door.

Braden watched her go, then he focused his attention on the line of customers backed up at the registers.

R.K. Phillips Books was in the thick of the holiday rush. Bing Crosby and Dean Martin were in regular rotation on the store's sound system, as was a Frank Sinatra Christmas album that featured a children's choir providing sing-songy, background vocals on a number of old chestnuts. Whenever one of the tracks with the kids came on, at least one staff member would scurry around the front counter and into the back room to skip to the next track. Something about those sugary sweet singing kids set everyone on edge.

Mary Ellen however was *always* ready to blow a gasket. Loren and Braden had come to understand why Roxanne made it an unofficial policy to keep the store's manager away from customers during the busiest holiday hours. Yet somehow, she still managed to commandeer a register from time to time. The results were never pretty.

Once the latest rush died down, Loren and Braden had a moment to unwind. They were on the schedule together more and more frequently during the store's busiest season, but so far they'd managed to negotiate a delicate if unspoken truce. It would be hard to call the tension between them any sort of dispute anyway. How could you be angry with someone for having feelings that you didn't share?

"Are you going to dinner with everyone on Saturday?" Loren asked

"I'm not sure, Braden replied. "I need to wrap some things up before break. I can't believe how fast this month is going."

"Just ten more shopping days until Christmas," Loren said in a quiet radio announcer impression. "When do you head home?"

"Sunday."

"Will your father be there?"

"Supposedly. We'll see how long he sticks around this time. What about you?"

"I'm staying here in town."

Braden nodded. *Of course she was.*

* * *

"How is this the first time we've eaten at your workplace?" Braden asked Hank as he looked around.

The dining room at the Red Tomato was like something out of *Moonstruck*, with checkered plastic table cloths and red votives flickering between shakers of pepper flakes and ground parmesan.

Hank shook his head. "I don't know, man. We just always plan on Brownie's or Brick's."

"He's here?!" a woman's voice exclaimed from around the corner." I'll be right back!"

Hank and the rest of the table fell quiet as a woman in her late-fifties with a pile of jet black hair and heavy makeup rushed toward their table.

"Hank!" she shouted. "They said you were here with your friends. I just wanted to meet everyone and say hello before you take off for the holidays."

"Hey, Elaine," Hank said as he got to his feet. "Guys, this is my boss."

"What am I going to do through the holidays without my best cook in the kitchen?" Elaine asked as she grabbed his face and smothered his cheeks in kisses. "Sit down, sit down. Now tell me who everyone is."

Hank went around the table, introducing Loren and Cole, Braden, Brooke, Elissa, and Hannah.

"And this is my girlfriend-"

"Hannah! Nice to meet you. The girls and I were beginning to think you were someone Hank had made up to avoid all the passes we're always making at him."

No sooner did the words escape her rouged lips, than Elaine burst out laughing.

"Nope, I'm real. And I am his girlfriend," Hannah said awkwardly. "At least for now…"

"I'm just teasing!" Elaine exclaimed as she squeezed Hannah's shoulder. "You are one lucky girl, we just *love* this guy! At any rate, wonderful to meet all of you. Happy holidays! And please, come back more often." She slapped Hannah on the back and shouted into the kitchen as she left. "Victoria! Get out here and give Hank and his friends some water!"

Hannah massaged her shoulder in pain. "Boy, she really likes you. Maybe *that's* why you never bring us in here. You're afraid I'll get jealous."

"Yes, because you should really be concerned about an Italian grandmother stealing me away," Hank said.

A tall, thirtysomething blonde in a lowcut shirt with billowing sleeves stepped out of the kitchen and began filling their glasses with ice water. "Hi, Hank," she purred.

"Oh, hey Vicky."

Victoria smiled at everyone at the table, her gaze lingering just a split second longer on Hannah before she departed.

"Holy shit," Elissa muttered from the end of the table. "Was that the St. Pauli Girl?"

Hannah fixed Hank in her gaze. "*Now* I see why you never bring us here."

"What, because of Vicky?" Hank asked. "She's just a friendly coworker."

"How friendly exactly?"

"You're kidding, right?" He laughed and waved her off, but his eyes darted back in Hannah's direction a couple of times. *He couldn't tell if she was being serious.* "So, Hannah and I are both going home until New Years. And I know Braden is going to Long Island. Brooke, what are your plans for the break?"

"Me? I'm going to *try* spending Christmas in the city with my folks," Brooke said as she watched Elissa at the far corner of the table. The two of them hadn't really spoken since the night of that kiss, and it felt like Elissa was keeping her distance now, which was perfectly understandable given the way Brooke had left things in limbo.

Victoria leaned around the corner. "Hank, are you guys ready to order?"

"I think we may need a few more minutes," Hank replied.

"Take all the time you need, honey."

Hank turned around to find Hannah giving him a withering look.

"How are you getting to the city?" Braden asked Brooke as Hank and Hannah took a prickly sidebar.

"The train. What about you?"

"Same. Train to the city, then another out to the island. Any chance you want some company?"

"That would be nice actually."

"Any plans for the break?"

"Honestly, I don't know. I don't really keep in touch with anyone back home anymore."

"Me neither. Maybe we should exchange numbers."

"Totally." She took out a pen and paper.

"It's funny," Braden said as they swapped contact information, "but whenever I head home now, I feel like my *real* life is the one I'm leaving here in Grimwood. Does that sound weird?"

Brooke shook her head. "Not at all. I feel the same way."

* * *

Brooke was alone in the dorm room while she packed, but she'd left the door open. The pre-holiday atmosphere on the floor was intoxicating as people ran up and down the halls, saying their goodbyes, exchanging gifts, and occasionally shutting their doors for more intimate farewells. The excitement in the air was refreshing. She hoped Loren would stop by before she left for the train station in the morning.

There was a tap on the door behind her.

"Knock. Knock."

Brooke turned to see Cathie Pepper standing in the doorway.

"Hey," Brooke said as she hurried over and gave her a hug. "Are you leaving soon?"

"Tomorrow morning." She noticed a gift in Cathie's hands. "Will you be there the whole break?"

"I'm gonna see how it goes."

Cathie nodded. She knew how things were between Brooke and her parents. "Well, if anything changes and you want to come back early, you always have a place at the house. You'll be happy to know I finally got the lights up."

"You did? That's great. Maybe I can help you with them next year."

"I'd like that," Cathie said. She lifted the gift in her hands. "I got you a little something for your trip."

"I feel bad, I haven't done any Christmas shopping yet," Brooke said as she accepted the gift.

"Don't worry about it. You have enough going on."

Brooke pulled open the giftwrap to find a brightly colored patchwork hat and a pair of matching gloves. "Oh, they're just like Jason's," she said with a smile.

"Yeah, I just keep making them. Old habits die hard."

Brooke pulled them on. "I love them. Thank you, Cathie."

"You've very welcome." A fleeting sadness flashed across Cathie's face, then it was gone. She smiled warmly. "Listen. Have you given any thought to what we discussed at Thanksgiving?"

"I have."

"I just want you to know that I'm serious about that. And believe me, I'm working on the same things myself. Just know that if you're ready to move on- Not move on, that's the wrong word." She paused to gather her thoughts. "If there's anyone you finding *appealing*, and you think you're ready, you should go for it. There's no reason to feel guilty about anything."

Brooke swallowed hard and nodded her understanding.

"You're alive. And love is for the living, right?"

Brooke's eyes welled up. "Thank you."

"That said, are you traveling alone?"

"Actually, no. I'm going with Braden."

"Oh *really?*"

Brooke gave her a look. "Didn't we discuss that already?"

"I know, I know," Cathie laughed. "I just think *one* of you should nab that boy while you can."

7.

IT WAS STRANGE TO be home again. Brooke lay in the dim quiet of her childhood bedroom, listening to the muffled sounds of traffic on the streets below. She looked at the lights twinkling through the icy window panes by her bed, reached out her hand, and drew a heart in the condensation that had gathered on the glass. Then she lay back, feeling foolish, and thinking of Elissa.

Brooke wondered where she was at this moment. Somewhere in Tacoma, Washington. Clear on the other side of the country.

Was she alone?

Did she have someone special back home?

Brooke rolled onto her chest, hoping the weight of her body would crush the ache in her stomach as she pressed her face into her pillow.

* * *

It was a pleasant surprise to see the wine *wasn't* something swiped from an event at the store. Cole set the cork on the counter and poured two tall glasses of red. He slid one over to her and they clinked glasses.

"Merry Christmas."

"Merry Christmas," Loren said before they each took a sip. "This is good. What is it?"

"Nice, right?" Cole walked around the counter and wrapped his arms around her. "When do you want to open presents?"

Loren looked around Cole's attic apartment, which was looking especially festive and cozy. He had set up a small Christmas tree, and the lights cast the room in a warm, multicolored glow as snowflakes drifted past the window. She couldn't have asked for a more inviting and romantic atmosphere.

"No presents until tomorrow morning," she said.

"But… in my family we always open something small on Christmas Eve. To help make the wait easier."

"Easier?" Loren turned around and kissed him. "You're like a little boy, you know that?"

Cole smiled, but the corner of his mouth hooked up just a little, as if he'd been told that many times before, and not necessarily as a good thing. "You don't want to open *anything?* Just for fun?"

"I want to wait!"

"All right, fine."

Cole's arms dropped to his sides, and Loren couldn't help but crack a smile. "You really want to open something, don't you?"

An embarrassed look came over him. "Yeah."

"OK. I want to save my gifts, but I have a little something for you."

Loren crossed the room and picked up her book bag. She opened the top and rummaged through a number of wrapped packages tucked inside. There were two for Cole – one large, one small – as well as something for his parents, and a heavier package for Braden: a leather-bound chap book she'd come across in the fall and thought he would appreciate. Then things had gotten awkward again, and she'd shied away from giving it to him. Now, after a romantic evening with Cole, the sight of Braden's undelivered gift made her feel guilty.

What was she doing buying something for another guy?

Was she keeping Braden on the hook? And if so, why?

Maybe it was good she hadn't given it to him. Unfortunately, she'd also inscribed it, so she couldn't exactly return it for a refund either. But that was a concern for another day.

She pushed Braden's gift to the bottom of the bag, took out the two packages for Cole, and walked slowly across the room, enjoying the twinkle in his eyes as he waited expectantly.

***

The train clattered over the tracks as Braden rode into the city. The seats around him were alive with energy, as New Year's revelers chattered excitedly, hammering out their plans for the evening. The few people riding to Grand Central alone busied themselves with newspapers and magazines recapping the year's top stories.

Braden wasn't reading. His mind was turned inward.

This Christmas had gone better than the year before. His father had actually shown up this time – arriving just before Olga served Christmas Eve dinner – and giving the vague suggestion that he might stick around past January 1st. Braden knew better than to count on it though. He'd long since given up on trying to understand his father's priorities.

This morning, before David McNutt could pull one of his famous disappearing acts on his son, Braden had asked Olga for a ride to the station, hugged her goodbye, and headed into the city to meet Brooke. For once, his father could get a taste of what it was like to be left behind on a national holiday.

Braden was a little apprehensive about hanging out with Brooke. He'd always thought of her as more Loren's friend than his own, but the closer he got to the city, the more excited he became. It would be nice to spend an evening wandering New York with a friend. He was looking forward to getting to know her a little better.

He briefly wondered what Loren might be doing for New Year's Eve, but did his best to push the thought out of his mind.

~

Brooke headed down the steps to the main floor at Grand Central. She glanced up at the split-flap boards as they cycled through the schedules. Braden's train had arrived, he should be coming up the ramp any minute.

She'd been pleasantly surprised when he followed through on the suggestion that they get together over the break. After spending the better part of the last week completely alone, it would be nice to hang out with a friend again.

The station was bustling with New Year's revelers. Brooke prided herself on her ability to whipsaw through New York crowds, but this was busy even for her! After bumping shoulders with several passersby as she tried to look past the oncoming crowd for Braden, she finally saw him, duffel bag in hand, walking through the crowd by the center booth.

He raised his hand in greeting as he got closer.

"We've got to stop meeting like this," Braden said.

"Happy New Year, Braden," she said.

"Happy New Year!"

They studied one another for an awkward beat, before an oblivious passerby swept past, ramming into Braden's shoulder and knocking him off his feet.

"Welcome to New York," Brooke said as she leaned down to help him to his feet. "You wanna get out of here?"

Braden nodded. "That would be good."

***

"Wow, no wonder the bookstore only charges cover price," Hannah observed as she and Hank mingled in the front room of the Phillips house.

"Digs like this don't pay for themselves, Hannah," Hank said. His eyes followed the sweep of the elaborate front staircase. "I still feel like a traitor being here."

"Why? Cole invited us. It's nice to do something fancy to ring in the New Year."

"We do fancy things," Hank said defensively as an older gentleman in a Glen plaid waistcoat wandered past, his thumb worrying a watch chain draped from his pocket.

"Hon, no offense to Lola's and that chicken gyro you like," Hannah said, "but that buffet over there is stocked with Beluga caviar and Moet & Chandon, and I intend to make the most of it." She headed for the food.

"See if they have Genesee!" Hank called after her.

He watched as she slipped into the crowd, then he surveyed the room again. A server came past with a tray of fresh salmon on Melba toasts. He helped himself to a bite and nodded contentedly.

Not bad.

He still felt funny being there though. Like he was breaking Braden's trust. He knew how Braden felt about Loren, and he certainly wasn't a fan of Cole Phillips – who struck him as a pretentious brat – but this was pleasant enough. He might even try some of that caviar…

The guests were definitely a change from the crowd on campus. Most of them seemed to be around his parents' age, but some were definitely of an older vintage – like that gentleman with the pocket watch.

"You made it!"

Hank turned to see Loren walking toward him. She was more dressed up than he'd ever seen her.

"Hey, Loren."

"Hank, it's good to see a friendly face. Where's Hannah?"

"She's casing the buffet. Where's Cole?"

"Roxanne wanted to talk to him about something. I'm sure he'll be back in a minute."

"How has your break been?" Hank asked.

Loren waved to Hannah, who was returning with a little plastic plate piled high with caviar. "It's been good," she said. "I almost hate to see it end... Have you heard anything from Braden?"

The question came so out of the blue that it caught Hank off guard. "No, I haven't. Have you?"

Loren shook her head.

Then Hannah was there, and the two girls were hugging and catching up. But all Hank could think of was the question he wished he had asked Loren the moment she mentioned Braden.

Why did she want to know?

* * *

They dropped Braden's bag off at Brooke's place on the Upper East Side, then headed out again in search of dinner.

The hostess at Rosa Mexicano greeted them as they arrived. Braden watched vapors of cold swirl from the melting snow on Brooke's shoulders as she requested a booth. He glanced to the side, where several groups were already waiting to be seated. Judging by the crowd, there was no way they were getting a table tonight.

He was mentally reviewing other restaurants they'd passed on the walk down – figuring which of them might have room if they circled back – when the hostess picked up two menus and led them through a doorway into the main dining area. A moment later, they were seated in a booth in a moody back corner, eating chips and salsa.

"Let me ask you something," Braden said. "How did you get us seated so fast? There must be a dozen groups waiting up there."

"I gave them my father's name. He was one of the restaurant's first investors."

"Oh. Well that's a good connection to have."

The waitress, a short brunette with thick glasses, stopped by the table with their menus.

"Can I get you two some drinks? Maybe a round of margaritas?"

"I'll have a coke," Brooke said. "He'll have a margarita."

"Oh, I'm good-" Braden protested.

"Better make it a double," Brooke added.

The waitress eye-balled them through her Coke bottle lenses and jotted down the order. "If the lady wants to get you liquored up, then she's the boss my friend." She slipped away and left them to look over the menus.

"I really don't need to have that."

"Braden, I won't turn into Judy Garland if someone around me has a drink. Besides, it's New Year's Eve, one of us should hit the hooch a little, especially if they're not carding."

He looked at her uncertainly. "If you say so, but I'm warning you, tequila turns me into a blabbermouth."

"Perfect. That'll help the conversation. What are you thinking of ordering?"

"What's good here?"

"The chile relleno is fantastic."

"Then I'm getting that," Braden said.

"So, let me ask *you* something. Is it my imagination, or are you not a fan of New York?"

"Pretty obvious, huh? Yeah, it's just not for me. It never has been."

"Aren't you from Long Island? I would think you grew up visiting the city all the time."

"Yeah. I used to come in with my grandfather, but that was different. He always took the lead and showed me around. But when it's just me, I get…"

"Get what?"

"It sounds stupid to say this, but I guess I get sort of scared."

"Yeah, that's pretty dumb."

"Thanks a lot! You can't *try* to make me feel better?"

Brooke shrugged. "What do you want from me, I'm a New Yorker, I can't feign sympathy for you country mice."

"In my defense, I can find my way around well enough, I'm not Alvy Singer or anything, but I'm semi-competent."

"You're like Alvy in L.A."

"*Exactly!* Panicked, but self-reliant up to a point. And with a 72-hour window before I go crazy."

"*Oh,*" Brooke pretended to look at her watch. "And how long are you planning to be in town?"

"Don't worry, I'm guessing I'll be out of here in 24."

The waitress arrived with their drinks, setting them on the table with a *thunk*. Braden rubbed his thumb in the chilled condensation on the side of his glass as she took their orders. After she left, he raised his margarita and gave Brooke one last look that seemed to ask '*are you sure?*'

"Enjoy it," she said. "Maybe it'll hold back the big city insanity a little longer."

"It's worth a shot," he said. Then he took a big sip.

"Good?"

He exhaled and wiped his mouth. "Not too shabby."

"So, why did you enjoy the city with your grandfather, but not now?"

"Everything was better with Pops. We were buddies. Coming to the city and scouring the bookstores was one of our things."

His eyes dropped, just slightly, but enough that Brooke decided to shift gears.

"Where is your family from?" she asked.

"They're all from here. Well, my grandparents were, and my dad is. My mother was actually from New Mexico, but she and my dad got together here I think."

"You think?"

"I don't really know my mother at all, or really my father for that matter."

"Oh."

There was more to Braden than met the eye.

"But you know she's from New Mexico," Brooke continued. "Isn't Loren from out there too?"

"Loren's from Colorado."

"Where is she now?" Brooke asked.

"Loren?" He flashed an evasive smile.

"Your *mom*. That drink couldn't have hit you that fast."

"I really have no idea. She might be back out there for all I know."

"I'm sorry. I shouldn't be so nosy."

"I don't mind. Friends are allowed to ask that kind of stuff." Braden dipped a chip into the salsa and took a bite. "Supposedly, my mom freaked out and left way back before I can even remember. She hated New York too. I've always kind of figured *she's* the reason I get so edgy in this place. Those southwest genes. My dad said she couldn't breathe in the city."

"Too polluted?" Brooke joked.

"Too confining."

"Like, space-wise?"

"Space-wise, status-wise. Those are my guesses anyway. There are a lot of social expectations. I take it you like it here though."

Did she? Brooke wondered. *She wasn't sure anymore.*

"Yeah, I guess I do."

Braden picked up on the doubt in her voice. "You might not want to join the booster club…"

"Some of the things I thought I liked about the city have changed since I've been gone. Or maybe it's just that I have. I don't really keep in touch with any of my old friends since I got my shit together."

"That might not be a bad thing, depending on the friends. How are you doing with that?"

"Sobriety? Fine. I mean… I certainly don't miss it. The stuff I used to do, and the people I used to do it with, just seem stupid since Jason. He got me straightened out. I've had a couple of slip-ups… but it feels like I'll be letting him down if I get too off track…"

"Do you miss him?"

"Of course. There are times I can't believe he's gone. We're about to start a new year, and he won't be here for any of it. That's so strange to think about. But then there are other times, when it somehow *feels* like he hasn't entirely left."

She thought back to that last time she'd screwed around with alcohol and pills. That night on the bathroom floor at the house party, when she was lying on her back, drifting in and out as the booze and bile churned in her stomach.

Don't throw it away, baby.

Jason's words echoed in her head. The soft, warm murmur of his voice.

Brooke thought of mentioning that night to Braden, asking if he'd ever seen someone he cared about after they were gone. The question was on the tip of her tongue as she weighed how he might react, but there was no going back once you brought something like that up…

"Anyway," she snapped back to the present. "I probably sound crazy."

"Not at all."

"We should probably shift gears before the waitress comes back and I start sobbing into the guacamole."

"If that happens, we can just blame it on the onions." Braden said. "Your parents must have been happy to have you home for the holidays."

"I think they liked *the idea* of having me home, but that's about as far as it went."

"What do you mean?"

"Let me put it this way. After lunch on Christmas Eve, they told me they'd booked tickets to fly down to Palm Beach the next morning, so I'd be on my own until classes started again."

"You're joking," Braden exclaimed. "They left on Christmas morning? That… sounds like something my father would do. Did they ask if you wanted to go with them?"

Brooke shook her head.

"So how was your Christmas?"

"*Unremarkable*," she said. "Yours?"

"About the same." Braden took a sip of his drink and pointed to the glass. "This is good."

"Voted best margarita in the city."

"I may have to get another."

"Just take it from the expert, drink them *slowly.*"

~

Halfway through his second drink, Braden took a turn for the chatty.

"No more of these things, OK?" He set down his mostly empty glass. "Any more, and… I'll be on the floor."

"You're rhyming."

"I *thought* I was!" he whispered in mock horror.

Brooke laughed. Once he loosened up, Braden had a charm she'd never noticed before. She could see why Loren liked him.

"So, tell me about Elissa."

Brooke nearly did a spit take. "What about her?"

"What's the deal there? Are you two friends? Are you in love with her?"

She studied his expression. He was being serious. No teasing. No judgment.

"What makes you ask that?"

Braden shrugged. "Tequila? I just get a feeling from you when Elissa is around. I thought there might be something there. Like, maybe you have feelings for her."

Brooke looked him in the eyes. The booze might have loosened his lips, but it hadn't dulled his senses. He'd seen right through her.

"I think I do, actually… Have feelings for her, I mean."

"That's *great.*"

"What about you?" she rebutted. "Are you in love with Loren?"

"Yeah. I am."

"*Really?* Even though she's…"

"Dating what's his butt? Yeah. That sucks, but there's nothing I can do about it, right? Isn't this sort of common knowledge with everyone?"

"I guess so. But no one ever talks about it. What is it about her?"

"Loren?" Braden peered down into his glass. "I mean, you know her. She's great, right? She's warm, and smart, and thoughtful, she *always* gives people the benefit of the doubt, to the point of dating people like…"

"What's his butt."

"Exactly."

"Have you ever told her how you feel?"

"Unfortunately, I have. She's never told you about that?" He sounded surprised.

"She has, but I don't know all the details."

"Let's just say it didn't go well. And since I'm an idiot, I made the mistake of bringing it up *again* recently, which just made things worse."

"I'm sorry."

"Thanks. Anyway, I think we were just starting to get back to normal again before the break, so I'm back to keeping my stupid yap shut. Tomorrow's her birthday by the way."

"Oh *shit*, you're right. I should call her."

"If you do, can you wait until I'm gone? I'm not sure I'm ready to maneuver anymore awkwardness just yet." Braden cocked his head to the side. "What about you? Does Elissa know how you feel?"

"I think so," Brooke thought back to their kiss in the hallway. "But I guess I've been a little uncertain about things."

"Do you think she feels the same way?"

"I think she has a pretty good idea what she wants."

"Is it what you want?"

"I hope so," Brooke replied.

Braden polished off his drink and locked Brooke in his gaze again. "Well, all I can say is if you think you're interested, and you think *she's* interested, don't wait too long to tell her, or before you know it, she could end up dating what's his butt."

"Or *her* butt."

"Some kind of butt. That's the point. Some. Kind. Of. Butt."

Brooke laughed.

~

They walked the streets after dinner, strolling past shop windows decked out in holiday decorations. The cold was biting, and the avenues were slick with snow and ice, but the side streets were almost peaceful as they made their way through the Upper East Side.

"Have you talked to anyone else this week?" Braden asked.

"From Grimwood? No."

Brooke had *wanted* to call Elissa every day since they'd left for break, but even if she'd had her phone number back home, she wasn't sure what she would even say.

"When was the last time you talked to Cathie?"

"Right before I came home, actually," Brooke replied. "She agrees with you by the way."

"About what?"

Brooke remembered Cathie's comment as she stood by the door, preparing to leave: *Love is for the living.*

"Basically that if I'm interested in someone, I should go for it."

"She's right," Braden said.

As they neared 73rd, they could hear people counting down to the New Year. Cars honked their horns as they zipped past. At midnight, the rumble of fireworks erupted over Central Park to their left. Brooke and Braden stopped at the corner and watched the colored glow on the buildings as the sounds of the display boomed through the cold night air.

They turned to one another and hugged.

"Happy New Year," he said.

"Happy New Year, Braden."

8.

FROM THE LOOKS OF the place, Hank and Hannah had returned to town a few days early. Braden was relieved they weren't there when he first got back to campus. It was nice to have some time alone to decompress after the long train ride.

As he was unpacking his clothes, he came across the wrapped gift – a book of course – that he'd picked up for Loren before the holidays. Although things had calmed down between them before everyone disbursed for the break, he'd still thought it best to hang on to it for a while. Now, that even more time had passed, he figured it was safe to leave it for her.

Later that night, as he was headed to the library, Braden stopped by Brooke and Loren's dorm, and quietly leaned the brown-paper-wrapped present against their door with a note that read "Loren."

~

Brooke studied her roommate's back as Loren picked the package up from her desk and turned it over in her hands.

"When did he bring this by?"

There was no question who it was from.

"It was by the door when I got here," Brooke said.

Loren's thoughts flashed to her undelivered gift for Braden.

She slipped her finger under the edge of the paper and pulled it open. Her eyes scanned the inscription inside, breezing past the message and settling, briefly, on the words "love, Braden."

Her shoulders dropped.

"He really likes you," Brooke said.

"I know he does." She read the full message, then set the book down on her desk. "It's like he looks at me, but only sees the best parts."

"Isn't that what we all want?"

"You would think so, right?"

"Do you like him?" Brooke asked.

"Of course I like him. I just don't know that I feel the same *way* about him. He can be a little… intense."

"Let me ask you something. Last year, when Braden was dating that girl Kate, how did you feel?"

"I was… jealous," Loren admitted.

"Maybe that's something to look at."

"I'd probably just end up disappointing him."

"At least you would know, right? College is going to fly by. I mean, look at everything that's happened already. It's easy to worry about falling short, but eventually, all we're going to remember are the things we did, and the moments we went for it."

"Are you talking about me or you?" Loren joked.

"I'm talking about *both* of us." Brooke said firmly. The thought had not escaped her that Elissa was likely back at school now as well.. "People fuck around too much, thinking they have all the time in the world, but life doesn't just fall into place. We have to go after the things we want, we can't just hope they happen for us."

"Maybe you're right," Loren conceded. "*You've* certainly come back to campus on a mission."

"Well, I did spend New Year's with Braden," Brooke replied. "You said it yourself. He can be pretty intense."

* * *

Brooke's heart was pounding in her chest as she approached Elissa and Hannah's room. She ran her fingers through her hair anxiously.

With any luck, Hannah wouldn't be there and they would have the room to themselves to talk. What exactly she would *say* was anybody's guess.

Would she ask Elissa if she was seeing anybody? Tell her how new this was for her? Maybe Elissa would open the door and Brooke would immediately realize she was over her. Wouldn't that be convenient? Complications and emotions wiped aside. Back to life and back to reality. But that was never really the case.

How had it happened with Jason? She could still picture their first kiss. But she couldn't remember *how* they'd gotten to that point.

Just knock on the door and take it from there.

Brooke clenched her fists with determination. She heard the knock, and felt the wrap on her knuckles, but everything seemed somehow two steps removed from reality. Then Elissa opened the door.

"Brooke-"

"Can I come in?"

"Of course," Elissa said.

Brooke stepped inside and looked around.

Hannah wasn't there.

"What's on your mind?" Elissa asked as she closed the door behind them. "How was your vacation?"

As Elissa turned around, Brooke stepped forward and kissed her. She dropped her hands to Elissa's waist, where she could feel the lines of her hipbones beneath her fingertips.

Elissa returned the favor, kissing Brooke softly, then passionately as they made their way to the bed.

~

"Think we'll get lucky?" Hank asked Hannah as they got off the elevator on her floor.

"I'd say that's a pretty safe bet," she murmured suggestively, her fingers slipping under the edge of his shirt.

"I mean about having your room to ourselves."

"There's only one way to find out," Hannah replied as she unlocked the door.

They slipped inside, leaning against the back of the door and kissing in the darkness before Hannah flipped on the lights. Then they turned around, only to jump back in surprise when Elissa rolled over to face them from her bed.

"Happy New Year," Elissa said blithely just before Brooke leaned her head up from the pillow beside her.

Hannah was too shocked to speak.

"Happy New Year!" Hank exclaimed.

Hannah mumbled an incoherent apology and pulled Hank out into the hall.

"I think I missed something," he said.

"Me too… But good for them."

"Should we head back to my place?" Hank asked

Hannah narrowed her eyes. "You bet your ass."

~

"There's something I've been wanting to ask you," Brooke said later that night as she and Elissa lay in the blue darkness together.

"What's that?"

Brooke reached her hand over to Elissa's left forearm, running her fingers down to the small tattoo on the inside of her wrist.

"What is this?"

Elissa raised her arm so Elissa could get a better look. "It's the tip to a drafting pen. Well, technically it's the nib to a calligraphy pen, but I thought it had a more timeless look."

Now that she knew what the image was, it was obvious. Brooke had used a similar pen in her classes the year before. Elissa's tattoo was in close-up, with the ink flowing from the tip of the pen and drawing a circle around itself.

"You know, I wish I knew where it was, but I *saw you* at one point last year. I can *distinctly* recall the feeling the first time you caught my attention, because I remember seeing this on your wrist as you walked by."

Elissa pulled the covers up over them as she leaned over and gave Brooke a kiss. "Then, I guess this was meant to be," she said with a smile.

* * *

Loren tapped her pencil on the side of her desk as she looked over her work. She was seated against the far windows, towards the back of Grimwood Library's second floor. From here she had a clear view of The Falls before they plunged over the edge into oblivion. It looked bone-chilling outside, and she was suddenly tempted to bail on Cole and walk back to the dorms for the night, but she didn't want to let him down. He'd actually suggested meeting for dinner at Ciao, which was out of character for him considering his general reluctance to pay for a meal out. She took it as a sign he was making an effort to meet her halfway on things, likely in appreciation for her accompanying him to so many uncomfortable family events over the holidays.

Loren checked her watch and grabbed her bag.

She'd better get a move on.

As she was slipping out of the stairwell on the first floor, she caught sight of Braden starting up the stairs in the opposite corner. He was lost in his thoughts, and as usual, was carrying what appeared to be a mostly empty backpack. As she slung her own bag over her shoulder, Loren made a mental note to ask him how he managed to keep his daily load so light.

That reminded her, she was still carrying her gift for him around in her bag. She hadn't yet decided whether or not she should give it to him. Either way, she needed to thank him for the book he'd left at her door. If she hurried, she could catch up to him.

Instead, she pulled her jacket tight against the cold, ducked outside, and headed downtown to have dinner with her boyfriend.

~

"I have something for you," Cole said as he pulled an envelope from his coat pocket and set it on the table.

"What's that?" Loren asked.

He slid it toward her.

"A gift certificate to a ski lodge in Vermont. My mother won it in a silent auction last night, then realized she couldn't go."

"Why can't she go?"

"She's doesn't like skiing," Cole said, "And she's terrified of deer."

Loren couldn't tell if he was joking. "So… she gave it to you?"

"That's right."

She opened the envelope and looked it over. "This place is *big.*"

"I was thinking we could take your friends with us."

"Seriously?"

This seemed out of character.

"Yeah." He nodded.

"*All* of them? That's a lot of people, Cole. It doesn't exactly sound like something you would enjoy."

"It'll be fun. A bunch of us up in the mountains, in a big lodge. If I need a break, we can slip off to our room."

Loren wasn't so sure. It sounded like a recipe for problems. Especially if Braden came with them.

"For real?" she asked. "I'm trying to see the angle."

"What do you mean *'the angle?'* I thought you'd like the idea."

"I do. You just don't usually like to get roped into group events like this. It's gonna take me a minute to wrap my head around it."

"I'm trying to be better about that," Cole said. "Sort of like a sort of New Year's resolution."

Loren flashed a tentative smile. "All right, I'll bring it up the next time I see everyone. When is this, anyway?"

"The end of next month."

~

"*Cole* wants to do this?" Hannah asked Loren skeptically.

"That's what he says."

She seemed unconvinced. "I don't get it."

"What don't you get?" Loren asked.

"We thought that dude didn't like to hang out with people," Hank said.

"He's hung out with all of you in the past."

"Yeah, and he seemed really agitated when he did," Hank countered.

"Have you been holding out on him or something?" Hannah asked. "Is this some tactic to get you up in the mountains so he can get lucky?"

"No!" Loren's face went red. "Nothing like that." She glanced at Braden's corner of their table at Brownie's, but he was focused on his meal.

"Did you catch him looking at some other girl?" Elissa asked as she squeezed Brooke's hand under the table.

"It *does* seem out of character," Brooke added.

"Yes. I know. My boyfriend is an antisocial pain in the ass, but this really *was* his idea. If you guys are interested, I'd love you all to come with us."

"We're down," Hannah exclaimed.

Hank glanced Braden's way, but his roommate was apparently willing himself invisible.

"Sure, why not!" Elissa added.

"I'm interested, but I don't have a *clue* how to ski," Brooke said.

"I'll show you," Elissa said.

"That sounds good, then put me down too."

"What about you, Braden?" Loren asked.

Brooke looked up and happened to catch Hank's eye. His roommate was waiting to hear his response as well.

"Yeah," Braden answered hesitantly. "I'll see if I can get the time off."

From the sound of his voice and his general disposition, Loren could tell it was just about the *last* thing he wanted to do.

"OK, then. So I'll tell Cole we have four yeses and one maybe." She was trying her best to seem enthusiastic. "This will be fun. It will be good for us all to get away from campus together."

"Especially after your visitor leaves town," Brooke added.

"That is very true," Loren agreed.

Hannah looked up curiously. "What visitor?"

"My mother is flying in for business for a few days next week."

Braden looked up, about to say something, but Hank beat him to it.

"What the heck is she doing in Grimwood?" Hank asked.

"That's my question as well," Loren said. "I guess I'll find out soon enough."

***

Loren was not a fan of Cole's car.

There was just something about Saabs that she'd never understood, yet they seemed to affect certain people like catnip. Her mother was one of them.

Cole's Saab was at least twenty years old, with orange, oxidized paint. The only thing worse was the interior, which was upholstered in custom red plaid that *must* have been Roxanne's doing back in the day. Loren hated everything about the car, so she suspected her mother would love it. That was good, since she'd be riding back in it shortly.

This was Loren's first trip out to the Grimwood airport, and the first time she'd driven since the previous summer, when Cole snuck a few too many chardonnays at an author event and needed help getting his vehicle home. Ugly as it was, she had to admit it was fun to take the controls of the old car. There was some serious power under that ugly, pumpkin-colored hood.

Loren was growing increasingly anxious as she got out of the car and walked into the terminal. Mary Beth Austin was a driven woman. Where Loren's father was laid back, almost to an extreme, her mother was always on the lookout for something that needed to be done, and she suffered no fools, *ever.* Those qualities had been invaluable in getting Puzzlebox Brewing up and running years ago, but as time went on, and the company grew increasingly profitable, it became painfully obvious that Mary Beth wasn't driven so much by success – Puzzlebox had been profitable for well over a decade now – as she was by anxiety and a continual sense of dissatisfaction. Loren's father described her as a workaholic, who was always pushing them to make another deadline or reach another milestone, the problem, as he put it, was that the goalposts were always being pushed back, so that what he *thought* was their final goal, was ultimately just a timeout, before his wife grew uneasy and began pushing for some *new* professional target.

Eventually, faced with greater success than he'd ever hoped for, and a wife who thrived in a continual state of discontented urgency, Rick Austin, in an act of self-preservation, had pulled back from the day to day workings of his business – as well as his wife – and the two of them began living largely separate lives. Loren knew her father had girlfriends, it was common-knowledge by the time she was in high school, but she was fairly certain her mother had her own flings as well.

She wasn't sure *how*, but Loren was certain her mother's unexpected trip to Grimwood was business related. The fact that Mary Beth would get to visit with her youngest daughter was merely a bonus as she worked on some new and ever-evolving business arrangement.

Loren could *hear* her mother approaching even before she rounded the corner at the arrivals area.

Click clack - Click clack

Her shoes clicked over the commercial flooring like a drum major's heals at the front of a marching band. Seconds later, Mary Beth Austin rounded the corner, sunglasses atop her head, dressed as though she'd just marched out of a board meeting.

She surveyed the corridor, her eyes briefly lingering on the heavy-set guard by the double doors before she noticed her daughter waiting for her.

"Loren!"

"Hey Mom," Loren said as they hugged. "Good to see you."

"Good to see you, too. I was afraid I wouldn't recognize you."

"It hasn't been *that* long."

"No?" Mary Beth asked as she looked her daughter up and down.

"How was your flight?"

"Bumpy. I didn't realize I'd be the only person on that little plane. I swear I could hear my bag rolling back and forth beneath me in the cargo hold. I hope it's in one piece."

"Well, let's get to the baggage claim and find out."

~

The Saab's engine rumbled as they pulled off Airport Road and headed toward the university.

"Where are you staying, Mom?"

"I *assumed* with you."

Loren whipped her head around, *"What?"*

"Relax, I'm kidding. But do you have to sound quite so alarmed?"

"Sorry, I'm just a little-"

"I like this car," Mary Beth interrupted. "This is what's his names?"

"Cole's. Yeah. He couldn't make it, but hopefully you can meet him tonight."

"And, does he go to Grimwood as well?"

"Sort of."

"Sort of how?"

"He takes classes now and then, but he's not really enrolled in a specific program."

Mary Beth exhaled. "What kind of classes?"

"I don't know, Mom. Should I get you a copy of his transcript?"

"I'm just making conversation. Loren."

"So, where *are* you staying?"

"Do you know the Claremont?" She unfolded a sheet of paper with the reservation and handed it to Loren.

"Oh yeah, I know where that is."

"It looked like it might be close to the school and my meetings and things."

"What are you here for again?"

Mary Beth flipped down her sun visor and started touching up her makeup in the mirror. "I just have some business appointments. And of course I wanted to see you and your school and things."

"What kind of appointments?"

Loren's mother flipped the visor back up and turned to her. "I'll tell you about it later. Now, will Cole be able to join us for dinner? I'd like to meet this boy who has kept you away from home for the last year."

"He's going to try to make it. He's supposed to work tonight."

"At the store? Does he work there full time?"

"Not exactly."

"Hmm."

Loren was pretty sure she knew what that sound meant, but she tried to ignore it. Instead, she tightened her grip on the steering wheel and jammed her foot down on the accelerator.

~

The Claremont Hotel was alarmingly close to Cole's apartment. After they'd gotten Mary Beth checked into her room and brought her bags upstairs, Loren parked the Saab on the street in front of Cole's building, and she and her mother started for campus.

Wind and snow whipped down the side streets as they reached The Ave.

"And I thought it got cold in Colorado! Is it always like this?" Mary Beth asked as she pulled her collar around her neck.

"This is a little worse than usual," Loren hollered over the wind.

"Is that the store?!" She pointed at the front of R.K. Phillips.

"Yep. That's it."

"Why don't we duck in?"

"I was going take you by later. I wanted to show you the school first."

"If you say so." Mary Beth replied uncertainly as they trudged up the main drive to campus. Grimwood Library's tower loomed overhead, jutting through the sliding layers of darkening storm clouds.

After a tour of The Writing Center, and a quick stop at the library, they headed to the dorms. A group was watching Judge Judy in the first floor lobby of Esmond Hall as they walked to the elevator. Loren pulled her keys from her coat pocket when they got off on the third floor and headed down the hall to her room. A girl in sweatpants and a tank top walked by and smiled as Loren stopped at her room, fumbled with her keys, and accidentally dropped them on the floor with a clang.

There was a noise on the other side of the door, like someone jumping out of bed.

Loren exchanged a curious look with her mother. She reached down to pick up the keys, and heard whispering voices as she unlocked the door. When she opened it, she found Brooke sitting on her bed with her back against the wall. Elissa was sitting in Brooke's desk chair, trying her best to look casual in spite of her flushed face.

"Hey, Loren," Brooke said nonchalantly.

"Hey." Loren nodded at Elissa. "How's it going?"

A palpable tension hung in the air.

Brooke looked to the door where Mary Beth was standing. "Are you Loren's Mom?"

"I am," Mary Beth said as she stepped forward to shake Brooke's hand.

"Mom, this is my roommate Brooke, and our friend Elissa."

"How does this weather compare to Colorado?" Elissa asked.

"It's a *lot* colder!"

Elissa laughed. "Good. So it's not just me! Brooke and all these east coasters keep telling me I'm weak, but if you say it's cold, then it must be *cold*."

"I still think you could toughen up a little," Brooke teased.

"How about we head over to my place, but you leave your coat here?" Elissa countered.

"You guys don't need to leave on account of us," Loren said. "We aren't going to be around long."

"Don't worry about it," Brooke said as she stood up.

"Yeah," Elissa added. "We were just about to go over to my room to get something…"

"OK, but seriously, you're fine staying here," Loren said. "We'll be out of your hair shortly."

Still, the girls grabbed their coats and continued to explain their reasons for needing to leave. Eventually, they both slipped out the door.

Mary Beth waited a moment before she broke the silence. "What exactly is going on there?" she asked Loren.

"I'm not quite sure. We haven't discussed that yet."

~

As soon as she opened the door, Hannah knew they'd need to make other plans.

She hadn't realized just how much she'd taken her freshman year single for granted. Now that she was sharing a room, and especially now that Elissa and Brooke were engaged in an as-yet-unacknowledged relationship, competition for their dorm room had become fierce, and more often than not, when she and Hank made plans to get together at her place, they were arriving to find the room had already been claimed by another couple. What's more, with the temperatures plunging at night, when he didn't have classes or work, Braden was spending more time than usual in his dorm, forcing Hank and Hannah to get creative.

Hannah eyed the two pairs of shoes on the floor just inside the door as she quietly grabbed the phone off the wall and slipped back into the hall to call Hank.

"Yeah, change of plans," she said when he answered. "Brooke and Elissa are here again. I'll have to go over to your place."

"About that…" Hank whispered back. "Braden is still here."

"I thought he was at the store tonight."

"He hasn't left yet. He's been at his desk all afternoon."

"Why isn't he at the library, isn't that where he's always holed up?"

"Well, this is his room, *too*. Plus, it's like 1 degree outside, he's probably sick of schlepping back and forth through the cold when he doesn't have to. I can't always ask the guy to go to the library, he's hardly here most of the time as it is!"

"Well when does he leave for work?"

"Pretty soon I think."

"Can you ask him to leave now?" she asked. She knew she was sounding desperate, but she really didn't care. "I just need ten minutes. Or *five!*"

Hank laughed. "You're turning the stereotype on its head. I thought *I* was supposed to be the sex-crazed one."

"What if we go to the radio station again?"

"That's just as far as the library, and there will be other people there this early." Hank said. "You know… we *might* want to start looking for an apartment together."

The line went quiet.

"Are you still there?" he asked.

"You think we ought to?"

"Why not? We could probably find something just off campus. Then we'd always have the place to ourselves."

"That could be nice…"

"Look, why don't you come over here. We can hang out a while, brainstorm ideas, and once Braden leaves for work, we can… you know…"

"I'll be right over."

~

"So, what are these business appointments you're here for?"

Loren and her mother were seated at a table in Lola, waiting for their drinks and Cole to arrive. He was unusually late meeting them, which Loren suspected was no coincidence. There were no events at the store that night, but he'd claimed the need to pick up supplies for readings later in the week. Loren was dubious. Her gut told her something else was at play, meeting the parents of the girl he was dating clearly wasn't something Cole was used to doing.

Mary Beth lowered her menu. "Do you know Grimwood Brewing?"

"Yeah. They're pretty big I think."

"They're about to get a whole lot bigger. They agreed to be acquired by Poptop Distributing six months ago, and I wanted to come out and talk to the founders to see what their acquisition experience has been like."

"Why's that?" Loren asked, though she was afraid she already knew the answer.

"Poptop has contacted us about acquiring Puzzlebox as well, and your father and I are considering selling."

"Really?"

"It was quite a generous offer."

Loren was shocked. "What about Dad?"

"What about him?"

"What would he do without the brewery?"

"Your father has no trouble keeping himself busy. Trust me. Besides, they've asked him to continue as head brewer if he's interested. Though I suspect he'd welcome the chance to move on."

"It sounds like you've already made up your minds," Loren observed. "What about you? What would you do?"

"I'd like to stay on and help take Puzzlebox national."

Loren was at a loss. She knew they were a mismatch, but the brewery was the only thing connecting her parents now that their kids were grown. Her mother was right, the chances of her father sticking around and following some corporation's marching orders were slim to none. He'd likely cash the check and increase his time on the slopes at Purgatory.

"I always thought you guys would hang on to the brewery."

"Who did you picture taking over eventually? None of you kids have ever seemed interested. You want to be a writer-"

"What about Patrick and Julie?"

"Come on. Can you really picture either of them running a brewery? Trust me, this is the right move, for all of us..."

It was the right move for her mother, at any rate.

Loren didn't know why, but the conversation was getting her upset. She looked away, and was relieved to see Cole walking in.

"Cole's here," she announced as she waved him over.

"Who?"

"My *boyfriend.*"

"Oh, right."

The flurry of activity was a welcome distraction as Cole took a seat and their drinks arrived. Loren gave him a questioning look as he mumbled his excuses for arriving late. Not that she cared what he'd been doing, but the more he talked, the more his explanation sounded like bullshit, and the more disinterested Loren could tell her mother was becoming. By the time the waiter returned to take their ordered, Mary Beth had pivoted to her usual conversational fallback: Business.

"So, how long has your mother owned the bookstore?"

"About twenty-two years," Cole replied. "She reopened it just before I was born."

"Oh," Mary Beth said. "So you're older than Loren."

"A bit. Not much."

"How long do you see yourself working at the store?"

"I'm not really sure."

Loren braced herself for the onslaught of follow-up questions. Young men without clear objectives were not Mary Beth's favorite sorts of people. Especially when they were dating her youngest daughter. Loren was just preparing for the worst, when her mother changed gears. Damningly, rather than asking Cole anything else about himself, she was clearly more interested in his mother.

"Twenty-two years? That's a fairly short period of time for a business like that to build such an impressive reputation. Your mother must be something else."

"That's what people tell me," he replied.

~

When Mary Beth expressed her interest in checking out the bookstore on the way back to the hotel, Cole begged off, saying he needed to check on something at his apartment.

"Will I see you later?" he asked Loren on the sidewalk in front of the restaurant.

"You will," she reassured him.

"I'm sorry he couldn't come with us," Loren said to her mother as they crossed the street.

"He could have," her mother noted, matter-of-factly. "He didn't want to."

"He's just tired I think."

"Hmm."

Once again, Loren noted her mother's disinterest. It was one thing for her to express disapproval with someone. It was something else entirely when she didn't appear to find them worthy of discussion.

The store's front windows were aglow, the warm light spilling out onto the chilled winter street. The tables and shelves of books looked particularly inviting through the frosted glass. The bell on the door jingled as they walked inside, and Braden's head popped up from behind the counter.

"Hey," Braden said brightly.

Shit, Loren thought to herself. She hadn't realized he was working tonight.

"Hi, Braden."

"What a beautiful bookstore," Mary Beth observed.

Braden's head turned "Is this your mom?"

Loren nodded as her mother stepped forward and Braden came around from behind the counter.

"Mary Beth Austin."

"Braden McNutt," he said as they shook hands. "It's nice to meet you."

"Braden is in the Writing Center as well," Loren said.

"Oh, really? Loren has been talking about that place and what's his name since she was a kid."

"Alan Grimwood?" Braden offered.

"That's the one!"

"We have that in common," he said. "We're both fans. Which is good since everything in this town is named after the Grimwood family."

"That's true. Maybe I should read one of his books one of these days."

"You've never read one?" Braden sounded incredulous.

Mary Bath shook her head. "Should I?"

"No question. He's one of the greats."

Mary Beth gave Loren a look. If she was indifferent to Cole, it was clear that she liked Braden. "Well, where should I start?"

Braden led her to a shelf of books by the entrance to the café and began walking her through several different editions of *Revenant.* Loren listened to their discussion as she walked over to the shelving cart and flipped through some of the new arrivals. She picked up a book called *The Tactless Irreverence of the Porcupine* and flipped through the first few pages while she waited for her mother and Braden to return.

"Oh yeah, we just got more copies of that one," Braden commented as he walked back to the counter and saw what Loren was looking through. "It's a book club pick again."

"How is it?"

"It's a leaf blower."

"Oh," Loren replied and quickly returned it to the cart.

"I'm sorry, but what is a *leaf blower?*" Mary Beth asked.

"It's a category we came up with. A leaf blower is literary fiction that initially seems clever and insightful, but the further you read, the more it begins to drone on and drive you nuts."

Mary Beth laughed. "What are some others?"

"Let's see…" Loren said. "There's 'woe is money.' Those are exaggerated stories of poverty and substance abuse."

"That's the kind of stuff Oprah eats up. Where you can't help but wonder how much of it is actually true. One of the first giveaways is when the author goes on TV and has abnormally white teeth," Braden added. "Then there are the 'beach towel accessories.'"

"What are those?"

"Any New York Times bestseller with a sepia-toned photo on the cover and the name of a foreign city in the title."

"Oh! That reminds me. Cole calls those the Polaroid transfers!"

Braden's faced screwed up in deliberation. "That's actually pretty good."

"There are the 'shoe stands,'" Loren added. "Those are the coffee table books you see stacked a half dozen high in *Architectural Digest*, usually with a pair of designer shoes set on top."

"These are great." Mary Beth laughed. "You guys should write a book."

"Yeah," Loren said. "Maybe we should."

"At any rate, I can see why you're both in the Writing Center." She held up the books Braden had suggested. "I'll take these two Grimwood books and let you know what I think."

"Great." Braden headed back around the counter and began to ring her up.

"I didn't realize you were on the schedule today, Braden." Loren said.

"I wasn't originally, but I've been taking some extra shifts." He lowered his voice a little. "I think Hank and Hannah could use the room, if you know what I mean."

Loren wasn't entirely sure she did. "Because of… Brooke and Elissa?"

Braden nodded.

Mary Beth listened but said nothing as she dug through her wallet for her credit card.

"Which reminds me. I think Mary Ellen has you on the schedule for that big ski lodge weekend in a couple of weeks, but I told her I could take your shifts if you need me to."

"Don't you want to go?"

Braden hesitated before he answered, "It sounds like it's more of a couple trip I think."

Loren wasn't sure how to respond. "Well, I may take you up on that offer then. But if you change your mind, I can see if someone else can cover for me."

"It's fine," he said. "I'm pretty sure I'm not going."

Braden looked at Loren's mother as he finished ringing up her books. "With Loren's discount, that comes to $22.10."

"Thank you," she replied as she handed over her card.

Loren struggled to come up with something else to say as Braden swapped the signed receipts and slipped the books into a bag.

"Well Mrs. Austin, it was very nice to meet you. Hopefully I'll see you again next time."

Mary Beth smiled. "It was nice to meet you too, Braden."

~

Two days later, it was obvious which of the boys had most charmed Mary Beth.

"And Braden isn't dating anyone?" she asked Loren as they waited at the airline ticket counter for her early morning flight home.

Loren shook her head. "He was seeing someone for a little while last year, but no one recently."

"That's too bad. I'd hate for him to miss out on that ski trip with you all. And Cole is *definitely* going?"

"Yeah, Mom," Loren replied flatly. "It's his trip to begin with."

"I just thought if he wasn't there, maybe you and Braden could go…"

"Are you *serious?*"

"I just liked him. So sue me."

"I like him too, Mom, but…"

But what?

When she couldn't think of how to finish her response, she just dropped it.

"Anyway, it was good seeing you," Mary Beth said as she gave Loren a hug. "I'm sorry it was so brief. Will we see you in Durango anytime soon?"

"I don't know, maybe."

"When is spring break? Maybe you could come back then."

"I'll let you know."

"Please do. You might not realize it, but we *miss* you. It would be nice to have you visit more often."

***

Loren took the Anniversary Edition of *Black Robes* down from the shelf above her desk and studied the cover. She'd flipped through it several times now, reading through the introduction and the alternate ending, and always finishing with the inscription in the front of the book, her eyes settling on Braden's inscription.

She took note of the feeling in her chest as she reread his words for the umpteenth time; evidence of something she already suspected.

Loren set the book in her duffel bag and carefully tucked it under the layers of winter clothing. The fact that she wanted to bring it with her on this particular weekend, even if she feared Cole might see the inscription, partly answered the questions she'd been asking herself. She was looking forward to a getaway with her friends, surprisingly disappointed that Braden wouldn't be there, and subtly dreading the time she would be spending with her boyfriend.

That probably wasn't the best sign.

***

"What's that blue stuff?" Brooke joked as she pointed to the sky.

It was a beautiful, clear winter morning. Most of the gang, including Braden, was standing in the back parking lot behind Valentine Hall. Hank had just left to retrieve his car from one of the satellite parking lots. Luggage, grocery bags, and ski equipment were scattered everywhere.

"It really is nice out," Loren said. "It reminds me of Durango."

"It's like *this* where you grew up?" Elissa asked. "How could you leave Colorado for Grimwood?"

"Let's just say it's not all clear skies and fresh mountain air…"

"Now *that* I can understand," Elissa conceded.

"I don't know about you guys," Hannah said as she looked through the groceries. "But I am definitely ready for a little time away from campus."

Loren motioned toward the paper bags. "Did we get everything on the list?"

"I think so," Hannah said. "Now if my boyfriend would just get back here we could get on the road."

An engine rumbled at the end of the lot, and Cole's pumpkin colored car pulled into the driveway.

"That's not Hank's, is it?" Elissa asked Hannah.

"No, it's not."

"Thank *God*, I hate Saabs."

"That's Cole's car," Loren said.

"Oh." Elissa's face flushed with embarrassment. "I mean, it's a classic. It's just…"

Loren set a hand on Elissa's shoulder as Cole pulled to a stop in front of them. "Don't worry. I don't like it either."

Cole killed the engine and got out. "Everybody ready?"

"As ready as we'll ever be," Brooke said.

"There's a second car coming, right?" Cole asked.

Two horn blasts sounded right on cue as Hank stopped his car behind them. "Load 'em up" Hank hollered. "Who's riding where?"

Cole turned to Brooke and Elissa. "You want to ride with me and Loren?"

"Is that all right with you?" Brooke asked Elissa.

"Sure, why not?"

"So, who's riding with me?" Hank asked.

"I think it's just you and me," Hannah said as she opened the passenger door.

Elissa and Brooke tossed their bags in Cole's trunk and opened the back passenger side door. As soon as she saw the red plaid interior, Elissa broke into laughter.

"What?" Cole asked, annoyed.

Elissa continued laughing. "I'm sorry, but is this car from some sort of J. Crew partnership? Where did you get *plaid* seats?"

Brooke tried to shush her, but it was no use.

"I just can't," Elissa wheezed, trying to catch her breath. "I've got to ride with Hank and Hannah."

Brooke shot Loren a helpless look. "I guess we'll be in the other car."

Cole was visibly irritated as he walked over to get Loren's bag. Their eyes met, but she didn't say anything.

"*Stop,*" Brooke whispered to Elissa as they walked back to Hank's car.

"What was that about," Hank asked Braden.

"I have no idea, but good luck." He patted Hank on the shoulder and walked around to the curb. "Have fun you guys."

"Are you *sure* you don't want to go?" Brooke asked from the backseat.

"Yeah," Braden watched as Loren climbed into the Saab. "It's for the best."

* * *

"That was obnoxious," Cole grumbled as he stepped on the gas.

"Elissa?" Loren put her hand on his knee. "She was just goofing around."

His eyes flicked her way, then back to the road.

Neither of them spoke as they sped through town.

"Don't forget, Hank is following us."

"He'll be fine."

"He may be fine, but it would be nice if you'd give him a chance to catch up."

"OK," Cole said, checking the rear view mirror as they got on the highway. "Here he comes."

"Is anything else wrong?" Loren asked after they'd been on the road for a while.

She could see Cole's jaw clenching as his eyes surveyed the road, but he didn't say anything. Either he hadn't heard her, or he was ignoring the question. Neither would have been out of character. Just when she'd decided to drop it, he broke the silence.

"My mother had me over to the house last night to talk about stuff."

"What kind of stuff?"

"Like my plans for the future. She thinks I'm not going anywhere."

This was dangerous territory.

"What did you say?"

"I didn't have an answer, just that I was thinking of taking some classes again next quarter."

"And what did she say to that?"

"She said she wouldn't pay for anymore courses until I was enrolled full time and on track with a major. No more jumping from one program to the next."

"Well, that doesn't sound all that bad. At least she'll pay for them once you settle on something."

"She also said they won't be helping me with my rent anymore if I don't settle on something by Fall quarter."

"That seems like a fair amount of time. We can figure something out by then?"

"What do you mean, *we?*" Cole muttered. *"I'm* the one feeling the squeeze."

His tone caught her off guard.

"OK," Loren said flatly. "Good luck with that then."

"I'm sorry," he said, realizing a moment too late how he had sounded. "I'm just stressed out is all."

Loren looked out her window at the snowy roadway whipped past her view.

"It's fine," she said coldly.

But it wasn't.

~

"I *knew* there was something with those two!" Elissa exclaimed. "That explains it."

Hank, Hannah, and Brooke had just filled her in on Braden and Loren and the convoluted feelings that frequently derailed their friendship.

"She should *totally* be with Braden! Not with Mr. Tight-Britches in his Locust Valley Mommy-mobile."

"Well, come on," Brooke said. "You can't hold the guy's car against him."

"Have you *seen* those seats?" Elissa joked. "But seriously, Braden is so much cooler than that guy! Did anything ever happen with the two of them?"

"Braden and Loren?" Hannah turned to Hank from the passenger seat. "I've always wondered that myself, actually."

Hank took a deep breath. This whole conversation seemed like a bad idea, it felt like he was breaking his friend's trust.

"Not as far as I know," he said finally. "Brooke?"

"I don't think so either. They just hung out a lot at the start of last year. And I think he tried to make a move, but it didn't go anywhere. Then she ended up getting with Cole."

"How did *that* happen?" Elissa asked Brooke.

"I have *no* idea."

"They should *totally* be dating!" Elissa exclaimed.

~

The light was fading by the time they reached their destination. The driveway leading up to the cabin was covered with a layer of fresh snow, which briefly gave their vehicles pause. Cole's Saab made it up the hill first with the bare minimum of spin-outs, a fact Elissa found incredibly irritating, especially when Hank had to ask them to pile out of his car so he could get a running start up the hill under minimal weight.

Loren noticed the hint of a smile at the corner of Cole's mouth when Hank finally skidded to a stop at the top of the rise. That bothered her. But it was the twinkle in his eyes when the rest of the group trudged into view a few minutes later that made her feel defensive of her friends.

They talked amongst themselves – making stray observations about the beautiful location, the weather, and what needed to get done – as they unloaded the cars and carried their things up to the door. Cole dug an envelope from his pocket and extracted a key, which he slipped into the lock and turned slowly. The bolt popped free and he pushed the door inward, leading the way into the dark interior. It was pleasantly warm inside. Spongy carpet sprung underfoot. After some feeling around, Hannah found a switch and flipped on the lights.

They were standing in a raised hallway, one step down was a round table surrounded by green, upholstered chairs. Turned wooden bannisters separated them from the living room. A large stone fireplace took up the farthest wall.

"Holy sixties mountain house, Batman!" Hank exclaimed as he walked through the living room into the open kitchen.

"Excellent," Elissa enthused. "It's like something from *The Pink Panther.*"

Brooke, Loren, and Hannah exchanged bemused looks.

Cole on the other hand was all business as he dropped grocery bags off in the kitchen and headed back out to the car.

"Is he OK?" Brooke asked Loren.

Loren shrugged and followed him out to the driveway.

Hank and Hannah exchanged looks, and started sorting through the groceries.

"Dinner will take at least an hour, so we'd better get started pretty soon," Hank said.

"What are you guys making?" Brooke asked.

Hannah looked up from a can of pinto beans. "Hank's grandmother's chili. According to him, it's the best."

"It *is* the best," Hank said as he grabbed a bottle of beer and knocked the cap off on the edge of the counter.

"Can you not do that please?" Cole said.

"Do what?" Hannah asked.

Cole motioned to the counter. "That bottle on the counter thing. This place belongs to a family friend. I don't want to damage anything."

Hannah gave Hank another look as they studied the chipped, worn edges of the brown laminate work surface. This place had clearly seen its share of wear and tear over the decades.

Hank flashed an exaggerated thumbs up. "Will do, chief!"

But Cole was already marching away, taking a quick tour of the bedrooms as Loren tried to keep up.

The master suite was situated at the end of the first floor hall. The room carried on the theme of "mid-century tacky." A balcony with floor to ceiling glass doors provided an expansive view of the mountains. The room itself was equally breathtaking, but in more of a gag-inducing way. The round bed was set with a green, crushed-velvet duvet and deflated brown and gold throw pillows, the stuffing long since turned to dust. Loren peaked into the bathroom to find a round, gold bathtub and faux marble walls.

Cole tossed their bags on the bed. "We can take this room," he said.

Upstairs, they found a similar, slightly smaller bedroom that Cole felt would be good for Hank and Hannah.

Another room with a double bed was situated just off the main hallway, across from the living room.

Down a flight of stairs they found the smallest room in the house. It was decked out with bunk beds and multicolored ABC blocks, clearly outfitted for children.

Back upstairs, Cole handed out the room assignments.

Hank and Hannah headed upstairs with their things, then came back down to work on dinner.

"Brooke, I thought you might like this room," Cole said, indicating the doorway just to the side of them.

Brooke leaned in the doorway, looked around, then popped back out.

"Cool," she said. She was waiting to see what Elissa's room would be like.

"Elissa," Cole began, turning to the stairs that led down to the kids room. Loren stepped forward before he could start.

"*Seriously?*" she exclaimed. "No."

But Cole plowed on. "*Your* room is downstairs."

Elissa fixed her eyes on Cole, then turned to Loren with a questioning gaze. Loren shook her head *'no.'*

"Those are the rooms we have to pick from," Cole said. "If you don't like it you can sleep out here on the couch, but-"

"Yeah, I don't think so." Elissa interrupted as she walked over to Brooke, leaned in, and gave her a long kiss.

Brooke wrapped her arms around her.

Cole's eyes went wide.

When they'd finished kissing, Elissa took a casual look into Brooke's room. "This one will do just fine," she said without looking Cole's way.

The girls got their bags from the hall and carried them into their room, closing the door behind them.

Cole stood in the hallway, speechless, as Loren headed into the kitchen to help with dinner.

Hank was unpacking grocery bags and sorting things for each of the group's meals when he stopped short and looked around frantically.

"What?" Hannah asked.

"Did you already put the coffee away?"

"No…" she replied, eyes narrowing.

Hank rummaged through the remaining bags, but still turned up nothing.

"We *did* get coffee though, right?"

"I don't remember seeing any," Hannah said.

"I know *I* didn't get it," Loren replied.

"Shit." Hank muttered. "Does everyone else here drink coffee?"

"Forget everyone else," Hannah stammered, *"I* drink coffee!"

Hank turned to Loren for an answer.

"Yeah… I'd say there's caffeine dependency, and then there's this group. We're all caffeine abusers of the highest level. This could get ugly," Loren walked around the counter and started rummaging through cabinets. "Maybe there's some here already-"

Hank and Hannah joined the search, reaching into the farthest corners of the cabinets and climbing up on the counters to examine the top shelves. Hannah pulled down a disarmed, ancient mousetrap, and a very large, very dusty box of Lipton tea. Hank and Loren came up empty.

"Well," Hannah began, as she blew the dust from the tea box, "This has caffeine, right?"

"That won't even scratch the surface," Loren said. "But we can try it."

A beer bottle clinked in the trashcan, followed by the sound of Hank opening another Genesee.

"At least we've got plenty of beer," he said as he started slipping bottles in the fridge.

~

"I wish you could relax a little."

Loren stood behind Cole, rubbing his shoulders as he looked out the window into the darkness of the mountains.

"I *am* relaxed."

"No you're not. You're wound up. I can feel it in your shoulders. You seem like you're ready to start fights with everyone."

Cole had excused himself partway through a game of Trivial Pursuit, which, not coincidentally, he and Loren were losing. Eventually, Loren had followed him upstairs to see if he was coming back.

"I'm fine," he said. "I just needed a little breather from-"

He caught himself, but Loren could hear the unspoken end of that sentence:

-your friends…

"You know, inviting them was *your* idea, remember? We're supposed to be having fun."

"We *are* having fun."

Loren cocked her head at a skeptical angle. "Will you come back down and join us?"

"Yeah. For a bit, but we *are* going skiing tomorrow, remember?"

"Yeah, I know."

She knew he was trying, but his demeanor wasn't particularly reassuring.

"What are you thinking about?" She asked, taking a different approach as she stepped around him and looked into his eyes.

"Nothing really."

She set her hands on his shoulders, but when he wouldn't meet her gaze, she dropped them to her sides and walked to the door. When he *still* wouldn't look her way, Loren slipped into the hall without another word.

Elissa, Brooke, Hank and Hannah were waiting around the table when she came back downstairs. A fire was crackling in the fireplace behind them.

"Is Cole coming down?" Elissa asked.

"I think so," Loren said as she walked over and took a seat. "But we don't need to wait for him."

* * *

Cole never came back down, and Loren refused to try to persuade him again. The group completed their game, then the other couples slipped away for the night. Loren waited until they were ensconced behind closed doors before she tiptoed upstairs. Cole was fast asleep, breathing heavily on his side of the bed, as she pulled *Black Robes* from her bag and returned downstairs.

She replenished the fire, then curled up on a chair beneath a thick layer of blankets, and reread Braden's inscription to her.

A log popped loudly in the fire, and Loren startled at the noise. Then she flipped to her place in the book and began to read.

***

"There's no coffee?" Elissa yelped. "How can there be no coffee?!"

"We forgot it," Hannah explained, as she dunked a half-dozen Lipton teabags in a mug of hot water.

"Huh uh. No. This will not stand," Elissa muttered as she watched Hannah take a sip of the concentrated tea. "How is that?"

Hannah coughed. "Not good."

Elissa turned to Hank. "Can I borrow your car?"

"Sure," he said, handing her his keys.

"I saw a convenience store about a half-mile back. I'll see if they have a can of Folgers."

"Folgers. Is that the one with the burro?" Hank asked. *"What?"*

"You know, Juan Valdez, the guy with the donkey."

"Who gives a fuck?!" Elissa barked. "Brooke, you coming with me?"

Brooke laughed. "Sure, why not?"

"Back soon," Elissa said as they marched out the door.

~

Thank God he hadn't gone on that trip, Braden thought to himself as he arrived at the bookstore for his morning shift.

He dropped his coat and gloves behind the counter, flipped on the store lights, and started getting things ready for opening. Icy winter days were some of the best times to be working at the store. Everyone was happy during cold snaps and snowstorms, grateful to be indoors and warm, surrounded by books.

Braden took an armful of new inventory off the cart and began shelving. He studied the books as he slid them into place, his mind shifting into a sort of meditative autopilot, organizing the titles in front of him as he rearranged the mental puzzle in his head.

By the time he opened the doors to customers, he was feeling like himself again, and thoughts of Loren and Cole and the rest of the gang were nestled comfortably in the back of his mind.

***

Ski conditions could not have been more perfect.

Loren stood at the bottom of her most recent run, waiting for Cole to catch up. Once the coffee emergency was addressed, the group had headed to the mountain for the day, where the couples all split off for individual runs, giving Loren a chance to smooth things over with Cole without either of them explicitly bringing it up. He was still a wee bit prickly, however, so how things might go when the gang reassembled was anybody's guess.

~

"Well, *that* went downhill fast," Hank joked.

He was attempting to teach the group how to throw pizzas, but having very little luck. He'd brought enough dough from Red Tomato for each person to make one pie, along with one or two extras, just in case. Already, two dough balls had hit the floor and been thrown out before he could step in, and now that the extra dough was in play, things *still* weren't going any smoother.

"We're trying!" Elissa said as she made her third unsuccessful attempt.

Brooke and Loren were laughing at their own hopeless crust attempts.

Hannah – in typical Hannah fashion – was intently focused on the pursuit of perfection, which she wasn't quite attaining, but she was having the most success of anyone in the group

"You're doing fine. It's not easy," Hank reassured them. He pressed out a fresh disc and started demonstrating another way to stretch a pie, lifting the dough loosely in his hands and allowing it to sag toward the countertop as he rotated it clockwise with his fingertips. "If throwing them is too tricky, try letting gravity do the work for you. It works just as well."

With that, Cole, who had already trashed his first ball of dough after a mishap, set his second attempt aloft with equally disastrous results. He quickly clawed the dough off of the floor and started for the trashcan.

"No!" Hank yelped.

"*What?*" Cole exclaimed, his face red with embarrassment and irritation.

"I didn't bring enough dough to lose any more to the trash," Hank explained. He motioned for Cole to hand him the dough. "The heat from the oven will kill any germs, don't worry. Let me show you how it-"

"Look," Cole interrupted. "We haven't all had to toss pizzas to work our way through school." With that, he threw his dough in the trash, and marched out the front door.

Hank, at a total loss for words, looked around the group. Reassured that he wasn't the only one taken aback, he walked over to the fridge and cracked open a Genesee.

"No offense, Loren," Hank said, "but your boyfriend is a real prick."

Cole's Saab rumbled to life in the driveway.

"Yeah," Loren said as she got her own bottle of beer and knocked the cap off on the edge of the counter. "He can be."

~

Ultimately, though there wasn't quite as much as planned, they managed to fill themselves up on misshapen but delicious homemade pizzas. The mood around the table was tense at first, no one dared mention the blow-up earlier in the evening, but the atmosphere lightened up considerably as the night stretched on.

Cole returned to the house as they were halfway through a movie, and slipped upstairs without a word. Loren made no attempt to get up and follow him.

~

Loren once again stayed up rereading *Black Robes* after everyone went to bed. She was fully absorbed in Alan Grimwood's fictional realm when Brooke stepped out of her room and slipped into the kitchen for a glass of water.

"You're still awake."

Loren looked up. "I don't think I can sleep yet."

"Me neither," Brooke said. "Something on your mind?"

"I think you can guess."

Brooke nodded in silent understanding.

"What about you?" Loren asked.

"I'm just… thinking."

"So, you and Elissa. That's pretty cool."

"Yeah," Brooke smiled. "I wasn't sure what you'd think."

"What do you mean? Elissa's great."

"She is, it's just… I can't help but wonder what Jason would think."

"He'd love her too," Loren said.

"I hope so," Brooke began. "I can't help but feel…"

"Not guilty I hope."

"No, not exactly. It's just this strange discomfort at moving on with my life."

"I think that's normal," Loren said. "But Jason wouldn't want you dwelling on the past. He'd be happy to see you with someone who treated you so well"

"That's pretty much what Cathie said too. But it wasn't until I talked to Braden about it that I made up my mind to go for it."

That caught Loren's attention. "You talked to Braden about Elissa?"

"I did."

"When?"

"Over New Years, when we hung out in the city."

A curious warmth bloomed in Loren's stomach, almost like jealousy that someone *else* could have a heart to heart with Braden, and not just her.

"I didn't realize you guys talked about stuff like that."

"We never have before," Brooke said. "It was actually a nice chance to get to know him a little better."

Loren blinked, bringing herself back to reason. "Yeah, Braden is great that way. He has a sense about things. What did he say?"

"He pretty much said to go for it."

"We all want you to be happy, Brooke."

The two of them grew quiet.

"What did Jason think of Cole?" Loren asked out of the blue. "Did he like him?"

"Jason liked everyone."

"But what did he *think* about him?"

"I'm not sure…" Brooke gathered her thoughts. "Like I said, he liked everyone, but he *cared* about his friends. Like you and Braden. So I don't know that he'd concern himself with Cole so much as he'd want *you* to be happy."

Loren took a deep breath.

"*Are* you happy?" Brooke asked finally.

"I don't know," Loren admitted. "I guess I need to figure that out."

* * *

Braden sat bolt upright, dropping his book as the dorm room door flew open with a bang and Hank appeared – soaked to the bone – luggage in hand. His coat and hat were flecked with ice and snow. Even his eyebrows appeared to be frosted over.

"So how was the trip?" Braden asked.

Hank held him in his gaze as he dropped his bags on the floor and stood there in silence.

"That good huh?" Braden laughed. "Do you need help?" He got to his feet and helped Hank pull off his sopping wet coat and hat.

"The trip *back*…was not good." Hank said as he nodded his thanks. "The weekend, for the most part, was ok, except when we were forced to hang out with Loren's asshole boyfriend."

"What did he do?"

Hank stripped off the rest of his clothes and pulled on a pair of sweatpants as he detailed the events of the weekend. When he got to the great pizza-making debacle, he grabbed a bottle of Genesee from the fridge, handed Braden another, and wrapped up with details of the drive back.

"By the time we got the cars loaded up, I didn't care if I ever saw that guy again. I just wanted to get back to Grimwood and do my best to avoid *any* future outings with him. But Hannah promised Loren we would meet them for lunch halfway, so I figured I just had to get through that meal and I'd be free of him."

Braden pointed at the dripping clothes draped over Hank's desk chair. "That happened at lunch?"

"No, *that* happened after we arrived at the rest stop for lunch, and waited, and *waited* for Loren and Cole to catch up. When there was no sign of them after an hour, Hannah told me to backtrack on the thruway to see if we could find them. Which we did. Cole's car blew a tire about ten miles into the trip back, and it turns out he didn't know how to change a flat, and he wouldn't let Loren get out to do it herself!"

"Why *not?*" Braden asked.

"Why doesn't he have triple A? I have no idea! But once we located them, the freezing rain kicked in, just in time for me to get out and change the tire for him. That was a whole other shit show, because the little donut in the back was flat too. So I had to drive back even *farther,* 'til I found a station that could patch and fill *that* for me. By the time I got back to the car, got the donut installed, and we were ready to start back *here*, it was after dark. Loren said they'd treat us to dinner when we all got to the rest stop we'd planned on earlier, but apparently Cole decided to just keep on going to Grimwood, because we never saw them again the entire way back. When we got to campus, Loren was waiting to apologize to us, but Cole had already gone back to wherever the hell it is that he lives. Can you believe that?"

Braden took a swig of beer. "Unfortunately, yeah, that sounds just like him. So I take it you won't be planning any follow-up outings with them?"

"No," Hank said as he finished his beer and immediately reached for another. "I most *definitely* will not."

***

Brooke and Loren didn't bother with a post-mortem after the ski trip. There was no question how the weekend had gone.

The most telling change once they all settled into their mid-winter routines, was the fact that Loren was around the dorms more than ever before. Other than classes and her shifts at the store, she didn't seem to be spending *any* time away from the room. The change was nice for their friendship, but perhaps a bit harder on Hank and Hannah, since Brooke and Elissa were spending much more time in Elissa and Hannah's room now that Loren was around so often.

The weather was further complicating the ongoing game of musical dorms, as a string of snowstorms increasingly kept Braden on the residential side as well, making Braden and Hank's place a less-reliable plan B.

The last time Brooke had been in Elissa's room, she'd noticed a sheet of apartment listings sitting on Hannah's desk. No one had broached the topic of changing the housing arrangements, but she assumed it was only a matter of time before someone brought it up.

***

"So how many inches are they forecasting *this* time?"

Braden handed his meal card to the cashier at Brownie's, and waited for the charge to go through. They'd been making small talk about the relentless procession of snowstorms for weeks now.

"Guy on channel 5 says a foot," she said as she returned his card. "But you know how *that's* been going. Whatever they predict, we get double!"

Braden shook his head in resignation as he picked up his tray. "Have a good one."

He looked out over the bustling dining hall. Brownie's was packed day in and day out now, with everyone sticking close to the dorms if they didn't absolutely have to be on the academic side. There was a sense of excitement at the severity of the weather, combined with the inevitable restless energy that comes with hundreds of twenty somethings cooped up inside for weeks on end. The air was thick with humidity from wet boots and drying clothes. The echoes of overlapping conversations fueling the din that rumbled through the room.

Braden was about to take a seat at a long communal table, when he caught sight of Loren reading on the other side of the room. She was seated in the booth where they'd tackled much of the work on their aborted writing collaboration, before a non-writing disagreement had caused Loren to throw all of their work in the trash. Now it seemed they'd come full circle, the same issue having flared up and died down yet again. They'd seldom spoken since the start of the new year, and not at all since the gang had gotten back from the ski weekend. In talking with the others, Braden got the impression Loren was around more often these days, but he could only speculate what that meant about her personal life.

"Mind if I join you?"

Loren looked up from her book to see Braden standing there with a sheepish grin on his face.

"Hey," she said nervously. "Sure. Have a seat."

"I'm not interrupting anything am I?"

"No, not at all. I'm just reading... for fun, not for school. I'm actually ahead on my classwork."

"I guess that's one good thing about this weather," Braden said. "There are fewer distractions when you can barely go outside."

"Right? This has been crazy. Aside from a few shifts at the store, and a couple of lectures that I absolutely couldn't afford to miss, I've just been holed up in the dorms."

Braden dismissed thoughts of where Cole might fit into the picture these days, but he couldn't help but think this new, solitary focus on schoolwork reflected a reassuring turn of events.

"I can't bring myself to go anywhere either. I like working at the library, but getting there and back just isn't worth it when it's like this. I do feel a little bad though, cause I *know* I've been cock-blocking Hank. Excuse the term-"

Loren laughed. "I've been doing the same thing to Brooke I'm afraid."

"What can you do, right?" Braden said as he crumbled crackers on his chili.

Loren smiled.

"What?" Braden asked.

"You're a man of routine, you know that?"

"I *do* know that, but what are you referring to?"

"You still get the exact same things to eat. You were crumbling crackers on chili every night we were here last year." She motioned to his side dish. "You still get a plate of pineapple. And let me guess…" she said, pointing to Braden's glass, "Barq's, am I right?"

"I like root beer. What's wrong with that?"

"Not a thing. I just think it's cute."

"I *am* pretty sick of pineapple though…"

Loren laughed. "But it works for you. You do well with routines. How is your writing going?"

"Actually, I just refinished something last night."

"What?"

He studied her expression and cracked a cautious smile. "My book."

"Like, *finished* finished?"

He nodded. "I mean, it still needs work, but if I stepped in front of a bus tomorrow, the thing is technically done."

"Braden, that's huge!"

"Well, I don't know that I'd go that far, but it feels pretty good."

"Are you happy with it?"

"It's a rough draft, but… yeah. I know that's going to change once I start revising it though."

"Still, that's a real accomplishment."

"What about you?" Braden asked, deflecting the attention. "Are you working on anything?"

Loren shook her head. "I should be, but I'm not. To be honest, I'm a little jealous."

"Don't be. There is so much more to life than hiding away in the library, making stuff up."

~

It was after dark when they left Brownie's, and the fields of white snow, combined with the swirling flurries beneath the campus lights, set off a glow that seemed to enclose them in their own little world, like they were walking inside a snowglobe.

Braden watched as Loren closed her eyes and leaned her head back, taking a deep breath, and slowly exhaling a cloud of fog.

They began a slow walk around the far edge of the quad, starting by Valentine Hall – Loren's freshman year dorm – and looping around past each of the residence halls as they conversed.

"I really am a little envious about your book."

"You shouldn't be," Braden insisted. "Like I said, as soon as

I start revisions, it's going to lose every bit of its imagined luster. And in the meantime, you'll have written something that *completely* puts it to shame. Then I'll be asking for your help making my little hodgepodge halfway readable."

"I highly doubt that."

"I *would* appreciate your help at some point if you're open to it though. I always appreciate your perspective. Would you ever want to read it and give me your thoughts?"

"Of course I would. Just tell me when you're ready."

"I will." Braden said.

Loren looked across the quad, her eyes settling on the snow-covered likeness of Alan Grimwood. "Have you witnessed any flares recently?"

Braden shook his head. "You?"

"I haven't."

"You wouldn't believe who was asking me about them a while back though."

"Who?"

"Think of the last person you could ever picture having an open-mind about something like the afterlife."

Loren thought for a beat. "Hannah."

"Wow. You're good."

"How did that even come up?"

"She brought it up one night last fall. Said she was walking on campus after dark, between the President's Mansion and the library, when two figures swept past her simultaneously and vanished. She didn't express the slightest hint of uncertainty that it had happened, she was just mystified by it."

Loren stopped walking. "What did you say to her?"

"I let her know I believed her."

"I wonder how close she was to the library."

"It certainly makes sense for it to happen around there, right? If a skeptic was seeking out a place that might change their mind, that would be at the top of my list."

They resumed their walk, rounding the corner by Hugh Lavery Hall.

"It's awful to think what happened in that library," Braden said. "All the people that were there, living their lives, working toward the futures they'd dreamt for themselves. Then some lunatic steps in and wipes them all away."

"I always think about the people they left behind," Loren said. "I don't know how do they go on."

"People are strong."

"Ever think of Cathie Pepper?"

"I do," Braden replied.

"I don't know how she does it."

"I guess you have to think, 'What's the alternative?'"

Loren stopped. They'd reached Esmond Hall, and the snow was beginning to pick up. "I hope I never have to find out."

"I hope you don't either," Braden said as he pulled his collar up around his neck and turned to go. "Have a good night, Loren."

"You too," she said.

Braden was already halfway down the walkway when Loren stopped and looked back. There were times Braden almost seemed like a flare himself. He appeared in her life suddenly, and vanished just as quickly. "Braden!" She called after him.

He looked back, his face obscured in a billow of fog. "Yeah?"

"This was really nice."

He was still for a moment, then he raised an arm, and continued on his way.

Loren walked through the dorm lobby, still smiling, but suddenly awash in uncertainty. Spending time with Braden *had* been nice. It felt natural and comfortable. Though they seemed to meet on the same wavelength only sporadically, when they *did*, it was as if they picked up right where they'd left off. Tonight – despite the snow and the passage of time – had almost felt like a continuation of that night all those ages ago, when they'd stood in the middle of the quad, and she had, to her confusion, rebuffed Braden's advance. And yet, in a curious way, it felt like no time had passed at all.

On the flip side, she hadn't been with Cole in weeks, yet it seemed like *years* since they'd last been together. And she had not missed him.

Loren's spirits were subdued, but her mind was tingling as she relived her conversation with Braden. The more she thought about it, the more she wanted to stay in *that* place. Whether that meant being with Braden, or spending more time alone, truly single and unencumbered, she wasn't yet sure, but one thing was suddenly clear:

It was time to end things with Cole Phillips.

She was already mentally dialing Cole's number into her dorm phone as she rode the elevator up to her room. For whatever reason, she had allowed this strange flirtation with a guy she didn't entirely *like*, stretch on long past the stages of a casual fling. Yes, he could be funny, and vulnerable, and there *was* something sexy about him, but Cole was also petty and difficult and driven by insecurity and ego. She didn't always feel good when she was around him, if anything, she was mad at herself for staying with him.

Yes. It was time.

The elevator doors opened and she headed down the corridor. Past the open doors, with Dave Matthews Band music tumbling out into the halls. Past the lounge, where the TV was playing

Must See TV. Through the thick of the late night college world. She psyched herself up to grab the phone, punch in the number, and end that stifling relationship once and for all.

But as soon as she rounded the corner, there he sat, his back against her door, his arms and legs pulled up to his chest.

"I'm so sorry," Cole said, his eyes shimmering. "I acted like a complete asshole. I want to make it up to you."

Loren stood and looked down on him. Then she took out her keys, unlocked the door, and let him in.

***

For the first time in ages, Braden was excited to be working a Saturday morning shift. The fact that Loren was also on the schedule might have played some part in his enthusiasm. He'd revised the first few chapters of his book, printed them out, and slipped the pages into an envelope, which was tucked under his arm as he ducked in the front door and made a beeline for the back counter. Loren was already in the back room, hanging up her coat.

"Good morning," he said as he took off his jacket.

"Hey," Loren said sleepily.

"I have something for you." Braden handed her the envelope. "This isn't everything, but it should be enough to get started."

"You work fast." Loren said as she peeked inside. "Say, what ever happened to that enormous backpack you used to carry around all the time?"

"It's around..." Braden looked confused. "What made you think of that?"

She seemed slightly dazed. "I don't know." She blinked and refocused her attention, tucking the envelope into her coat sleeve. "I'll look these over and get back to you as soon as I can."

"Take your time. It's going to take me a while to get through the bulk of it."

"I just don't want to slow you down if you've got some momentum going."

"Relax. It's not like there's any sort of deadline." He again noticed the severity of her expression. "Are you all right?"

"I'm fine. I think I just need some more coffee. You want some?"

"Sure. A fifth cup won't kill me, right?"

Loren started for the café, but stopped and turned around. "I *am* excited to read it, Braden."

"OK," he replied, a curious smile stretching across his face. "I'm glad."

Something was eating at her, but Braden was determined not pry.

9.

THE APARTMENT MANAGER, LLOYD, was 80 years old if he was a day, but despite his age, there was a spring in his step and a friendly glimmer in his eyes that made Hank and Hannah like him right away. He led them down the front hall of unit 304, then stepped to the side so they could get a look around the living and dining areas.

The Dean Apartments was a three-story brick building from 1927. The front, with its arched entry and tall center section, resembled a high school from a John Hughes movie. Lovingly cared for, with fresh paint, original hardwood floors, and most of the original period details, it was just the kind of place Hannah had been hoping for when she circled the ad in the classifieds that morning. The struggle for privacy was becoming more and more of a problem, and it seemed the only solution was to move off campus into a place of their own. They'd originally hoped to get through the end of the school year, but the tension over the last few weeks had started to get the better of them, so they'd finally starting looking.

"This unit has the original murphy bed," Lloyd noted, pointing to a set of double doors along the dining room wall.

"Very cool," Hank replied as he walked around a green, child's scooter and peeked into the bedroom. His eyes settled on a crib in the corner of the room.

"The couple that lives here at the moment has a young kid," Lloyd explained, indicating the scooter. "They've been here almost four years, but I think they want something with another bedroom now that their daughter is getting older. Really nice family though."

Hank walked over and joined Hannah in the kitchen. "What do you think?" he asked her. It was starting to dawn on him just what it meant for them to move in together.

"What do *you* think?" Hannah asked cautiously.

"Well, it's close to campus. It's near to the restaurant. It *seems* really nice. And it would give us our own space finally. It seems like it could be perfect.

I think so too," Hannah said. "I love it."

"How much is it again?" Hank asked Lloyd.

"$795 a month," Lloyd said. "That includes water and everything but electric."

"Does that seem do-able?" Hank asked Hannah.

"I think so. Just."

Hank turned to Lloyd again. "When would we be able to move in?"

"You could have the keys three weeks from today if that worked for you."

Hank looked at Hannah one last time for confirmation. She bobbed her head.

"We'll take it," Hank announced.

"Excellent!" Lloyd said as he pulled out a binder. "Let's get started on the paperwork."

* * *

"Behind you," Brooke said as she and Elissa hauled Hannah's steamer trunk through Taylor Hall's main entrance. They set it next to the boxes Loren and Hannah had already hauled down.

"Thanks again for your help," Hannah said.

"Not a problem, roomie," Elissa replied as she stopped to catch her breath. "I do have one question though… How did the four of *us* get stuck doing all the heavy lifting? Where the heck are Hank and Braden?"

"They're picking up the U-Haul," Hannah said. "But yeah, the timing *is* a little interesting, isn't it?"

~

"Is that a dead bat?" Hank asked as he poked a stick through the moving van's front grill.

Braden leaned in for a closer look. "It sure looks like it. I wonder if he ever saw it coming."

The little guy was spread eagle, his wings burned onto the radiator.

"Jesus, I hope that's not some sort of omen."

"Don't worry," Braden said as he walked around to the passenger door. "It's gonna be fine."

They rode in silence for a ways – Hank driving, while Braden watched the streets go by.

"You know, if you're having any doubts, you really don't need to move out, Hank. Now that the weather's improving, I can clear out more so you guys can have the room to yourselves."

"Nah. It's time. Hannah isn't so happy with her major, so I think she wants to focus a little more on us."

"And how do *you* feel about that?" Braden asked warily.

"Well… it *was* getting a little rocky over the winter. Not because of the room logistics – although that didn't help – just the whole thing with Hannah's project getting trashed. And Elissa having the same major sort of underlined how unhappy Hannah is in the program.."

"So… you're saying it's *Elissa's* fault. That makes me feel a lot better."

"No, Brady. That's not what I'm saying. Don't go getting me in trouble."

"Fine, but all kidding aside, you're probably smart to be doing this now, before we get closer to the end of the year and finals."

"That's what I was thinking. Get the move over with before everything gets crazy in a few weeks. Do you know your housing plans for next year?"

"I haven't really thought about it. I guess I'll see if I can get a single." Braden pointed to the pile of boxes on the curb as they pulled into the lot. "It looks like the girls have already moved the bulk of it."

Hank grinned. "Then we timed things perfectly."

All four girls crossed their arms and glared at them.

"They don't look so happy about it either," Braden observed.

"No," Hank said, his mouth flattening as he killed the engine. "They certainly don't."

~

It was late afternoon by the time they got all of the boxes and newly-acquired Goodwill furniture moved into Hank and Hannah's building.

Loren looked around the apartment admiringly between bites of pizza. "I like it. Anyone else know where they'll be next year?"

"Brady's sticking to dorm life," Hank replied. "We discussed it on the way back from the U-Haul place."

"Oh, is *that* why it took you guys so long to get back?" Hannah asked.

Braden laughed. "That, and we were hoping you'd get all the boxes moved before we got there."

"Mission accomplished," Brooke said.

"So, Braden is staying on campus." Hannah turned to Brooke and Elissa. "What about you guys?"

They looked at each other awkwardly.

"We haven't really talked about it," Elissa replied. "I guess I was waiting to see if Brooke and Loren were rooming together again."

Brooke looked over at her roommate. "And I was sort of thinking Loren might be planning to move off campus too…"

Loren was suddenly on the spot. "You mean, like… moving in with Cole?" Her eyes darted around the group as she decided what to say. "I… don't really see that being a factor next year."

Brooke studied Braden's face, searching for a reaction, but he didn't give anything away.

"Maybe the three of us could get a triple?" Elissa suggested. "One of those deals with three bedrooms and a living room in the middle.

"That could be good," Loren said.

Hank was also gauging Braden's response, and he was just about to jump in with a suggestion for *another* housing option for Braden and Loren, when Hannah gave him a look and shook her head *no*.

~

Braden and Loren were the last to leave Hank and Hannah's apartment that evening.

"So, our friends are all shacking up." Loren observed as they walked back to campus.

"I know. I feel like we should get them a toaster or something," Braden said.

She gave him a funny look. "A what?"

"A toaster. You know, as a housewarming gift."

"Oh, yeah, maybe we should," she said. "I'd go in on that with you. Maybe one of those make-at-home Egg McMuffin makers."

"I've always wanted one of those."

"Why does that not surprise me?"

Braden stopped suddenly. "You know, I've been meaning to tell you something."

Loren looked nervous. "You have?"

"I worked your suggestions into the book, and I printed up the rest of the pages if you're still interested in helping me with them."

She could feel the tension in her shoulders relax. "Absolutely."

"Great," Braden replied as they continued walking. "I'll get them to you this week."

~

The manila envelope in Loren's staff mailbox had no bearing on her decision, though her heart did skip a beat when she folded the top open and saw the remaining pages from Braden's manuscript inside. The truth was, from the moment she'd seen Cole's name on the week's work schedule alongside her own, she knew the time had come.

Cole had been calling and leaving messages for her the last couple of weeks, but between work, final assignments, and studying for exams, Loren hadn't found the time to call him back. And the truth was, she'd once again been feeling the need to call it quits between them. So, shortly before their evening shift began, she led Cole to one of the alcoves near the back, and told him quietly, but firmly, that this was it.

"I'm heading home for the summer, but I want to end things now."

Cole's eyes betrayed his indignation, even as his open mouth showed his outright shock.

"Are you *serious?!*"

"I am," Loren replied. "And I'll tell you another thing. Unlike some of your previous bookstore girlfriends, I'm not going to hang around here for a few weeks, then quit. I *like* this job, and I intend to keep it through the end of the school year. And next year as well. So let's keep things civil, shall we?"

10.

THERE WERE MOMENTS WHEN Loren understood Braden's habit of holing up in the library to study and write, and she couldn't think of a more fitting place to work on his book, than in the same study hall where Braden so often sequestered himself when he was deep in a project.

Other than the more hectic periods around finals, she'd been marking corrections and noting suggestions for the last few weeks. Braden's writing was so different from her own, and at first, she wondered if her personal preferences were too at odds with his style. But the deeper into his book she got, the more she felt her approach brought something valuable to the table. While Braden's writing seemed to swirl and expand like smoke, her revisions cut through the haze when necessary, excising repetitive passages and keeping the story focused and moving. It felt good to put her skills to work again. She was proud of her edits.

Loren had been going over Braden's manuscript for much of the day when it finally dawned on her that the knot in her stomach wasn't apprehension at the book's conclusion, or angst over the upcoming end to the school year, but a reminder that it was well past time to stop and get a bite to eat. She snapped the cap on her red pen, shuffled the pages together, and slipped them into her bag. Only the distant sounds of muffled coughs and moving chairs reminded her that there were other people working in the library as well.

Air hissed softly from the central air.

And Loren was suddenly awash in a strange sensation, a lonely sadness which she'd felt once or twice before, always during late night work sessions at the library.

Though it was a warm spring night, she felt a chill as she slipped into the long corridor outside the study hall. She glanced back into the room, making sure she hadn't dropped any loose pages, then she started down the hallway toward the stairs. Just as she took her first step, she was startled to see a girl standing alone off to the side of the passageway. Her face was the picture of calm, her eyes cast down at the floor. Loren stopped in her tracks.

"Oh!" Loren exclaimed. "You startled me."

The girl looked up slowly, her eyes meeting Loren's gaze as a peaceful smile appeared on her face.

Loren could hear her own breath in the quiet.

The girl continued to look at her, the expression on her face unchanging. That's when Loren recognized her. The blond hair. The gentle features. That same contemplative look, staring back at her through all those lost years.

She was a flare.

Deborah Payne.

The object of one unstable boy's obsession, and the first victim of Grimwood University's infamous tragedy.

Loren opened her mouth as she walked, struggling to force a sound from her lips. But all she could do was breathe slowly in and out as her heart pounded in her chest.

Deborah continued to watch her, the cautious smile frozen on her face as Loren passed by.

When she was within steps of her, Loren's pulse began to quicken. Panic was setting in. She hurried to the stairwell, all the while keeping her eyes on the flare. When she reached the steps, Loren paused to look back. Deborah was gazing down at the floor now, an expression of sadness washing over her face.

Loren started down the stairs, but stopped one last time. When she again looked down the corridor, Deborah Payne was gone.

* * *

They'd settled on Brick's for their final meal of the year. Not that there'd ever been any real question over where they would eat.

"Six Brick Plates coming up," Betty confirmed. "Anything to drink?"

"I'll have a mug of Pepto-Bismal," Elissa joked.

Betty's brow furrowed. She'd heard this joke a million times before. "How 'bout a round of Pepsis?"

"Sounds great," Hank said.

"Six plates of upset stomach," Hannah said once Betty was out of earshot. "This is a terrible end of the year tradition."

"It may not be much," Hank replied. "But it's ours."

Betty dropped off their food as they were discussing their summer plans.

"Back to Colorado," Hank mused as Loren shared her decision to return to Durango for the break.

"It just seems like a good time to get back and sort a few things out," Loren mused.

It felt in a curious way like she'd been living another life for much of the last year. She was curious to see how she'd feel after a summer back home.

"Well, if you get bored out there and want to come back early, you can always crash on the murphy bed in our apartment," Hannah said.

"That's true," Hank added. "It might cripple your back, but it's all yours."

"What about you guys," Braden asked Elissa and Brooke. "Anything big planned?"

"As a matter of fact, we just found a place around the corner," Brooke said. "We're going to stick around here too."

"Oh, good," Hannah said. "I won't be the only girl in town." She'd already announced her plans to take a few summer classes to make up for her partially botched year.

"What about you, Brady?" Hank asked.

"Me?" Braden said quietly. "I'm just… heading home."

* * *

"Boy, you sure don't need much, do you?"

"How do you mean?" Braden asked.

He and Loren were once again standing in the middle of the Grimwood train station. Just the two of them.

She pointed at his banged up duffel bag. "Two years in, and you're still traveling with that same bag." She motioned to her own luggage. "Meanwhile, this doesn't even include the stuff I asked Hannah to store for me until I get back."

Braden gave her a sheepish look. "I asked Hank to hold onto a box of books for me too."

"*A* box," Loren pointed out. "Emphasis on the *a*."

"To be fair, I have a house full of books waiting for me when I get home."

Loren wasn't sure what to think about that. She was suddenly keenly aware of the fact that Braden was returning to an empty house.

"Are you going to be all right?" she asked.

"Yeah, of course." He sounded surprised at the question.

"You can always give me a call over the summer, if you get bored I mean."

"You too," Braden replied. Then he laughed. "What will we talk about?"

"I don't know… Alan Grimwood? And I'll mail the rest of your book back to you by the fourth of July. I promise. We can talk about that."

"Sounds good."

They stared at one another awkwardly, unsure of the safest route to steer the conversation. Finally, the announcer's voice crackled in through the overhead speakers.

"The eleven o'clock to Grand Central is now boarding. All passengers, proceed to track fifteen."

"I guess that's it," Braden said as he picked up his bag. "What time is your train leaving?"

"Within the hour," she said.

"I can't believe how quickly this year went."

"It flew," Loren said as she leaned in to give him a long hug. "Take care of yourself Braden."

His eyes glimmered, then his gaze dropped to the floor. "I'll see you in the fall."

"See you in the fall."

Loren watched as he walked away and was quickly absorbed by the crowd of passengers slipping through the doors to the platform.

She stood in the middle of the empty station as the final boarding announcements went out and the sound of the departing train shook the station. The rumble grew stronger as the train, and Braden, moved farther and farther away.

She was officially heading home, but at the moment, it felt as though she was *leaving* home. It was funny how one's center shifted…

"Now boarding, the eleven thirty to Chicago Union Station."

Loren blinked and looked up at the clock.

She'd been lost in her thoughts as she looked back over the past few months.

"All passengers, please proceed to track seven."

She carried her bags out to the platform and climbed aboard the train. The whistle blew and the engine rattled the cars. Loren made her way down the aisle as the train pulled away from the station. She found a seat by the windows, where she could watch Grimwood recede into the distance. When they had slipped out of sight, she pulled *Black Robes* from her bag and began reading, once again sinking into the familiar pages as she made her way across the country and through the increasingly complex emotions swirling in her heart.

About the Author

Mike Attebery is the author of ten novels, including *The Grimwood Trilogy*, *Chokecherry Canyon*, *Firepower*, *Seattle On Ice*, *Bloody Pulp*, and *Rosé in Saint Tropez*. He lives with his family on an island off the coast of Washington State.

You can find Mike online at:
www.facebook.com/AtteberyBooks/

on Instagram at
https://www.instagram.com/mikeatteberyauthor/

and on his website http://www.mikeattebery.com